Here's w
L

MW01146832

"With an irreverent, tell-it-like-it-is, suburban-mom-assassin narrator, Leslie Langtry's *'Scuse Me While I Kill This Guy* delivers wild and wicked fun."
—Julie Kenner, USA Today Bestselling Author

"Darkly funny and wildly over the top, this mystery answers the burning question, 'Do assassin skills and Girl Scout merit badges mix…' one truly original and wacky novel!"
—RT BOOK REVIEWS

"Those who like dark humor will enjoy a look into the deadliest female assassin and PTA mom's life."
—Parkersburg News

"Mixing a deadly sense of humor and plenty of sexy sizzle, Leslie Langtry creates a brilliantly original, laughter-rich mix of contemporary romance and suspense in *'Scuse Me While I Kill This Guy.*"
—Chicago Tribune

"The beleaguered soccer mom assassin concept is a winner, and Langtry gets the fun started from page one with a myriad of clever details."
—Publisher's Weekly

BOOKS BY LESLIE LANGTRY

Merry Wrath Mysteries:
Merit Badge Murder
Mint Cookie Murder
Scout Camp Murder (short story in the Killer Beach Reads collection)
Marshmallow S'More Murder
Movie Night Murder

Greatest Hits Mysteries:
'Scuse Me While I Kill This Guy
Guns Will Keep Us Together
Stand By Your Hitman
I Shot You Babe
Paradise By The Rifle Sights
Snuff the Magic Dragon
My Heroes Have Always Been Hitmen
Four Killing Birds (a holiday short story)
Have Yourself a Deadly Little Christmas (a holiday short story)

Other Works:
Sex, Lies, & Family Vacations

Hanging Tree Tales YA horror novels:
Hell House
Tyler's Fate
Witch Hill
The Teacher

MOVIE NIGHT MURDER

a Merry Wrath mystery

Leslie Langtry

MOVIE NIGHT MURDER

CHAPTER ONE

———

Reverend Miller stepped up to Riley and me, smiling as he sprinkled us with holy water. Kelly and her husband Robert immediately took a large step backwards as I burst into flame. This is what I get for going to church.

I didn't really burst into flame. I had my suspicions, and apparently, so did my best friend and her husband, but I didn't so much as sizzle. I just haven't been to a church in…never.

"Nervous?" Riley mumbled to me out of the side of his mouth.

"Oh, and you're perfectly at home here?" I asked.

"Of course. I'm a Methodist, born and reared," he replied smoothly.

I had to admit—he looked completely at ease in this large Lutheran church in Who's There, Iowa.

"I knew I should've shot you dead that time in Kabul."

"Do we have an atheist in our midst?" Riley feigned horror.

"No. Just an avowed agnostic. I still can't figure out why Kelly chose me to be Finn's godmother, and I have no way of even *comprehending* why she chose you to be the godfather."

Riley didn't reply because at that moment, he was in the midst of handing my tiny namesake over to Reverend Miller to be doused with water. The two-month-old screamed in protest, flailing her fist in the perfect right hook that landed on the minister's chin. I couldn't help but smile. This kid was definitely a future spy. Maybe it made sense to have two CIA agents as her godparents after all.

My name is Merry Wrath. I was born Finnoughla Merrygold Czrygy, here in this small city in Iowa. I used to be a

CIA agent, but now I'm just a Girl Scout leader—a job that is infinitely more dangerous than being a spy.

Almost two years ago, I was outed by the vice president of the United States while still in the field. He was angry with my father Senator Czrygy's take on one of his policies, and *accidentally* turned my name over to the press.

The CIA retired me with a nice severance package, and I changed my name to Merry Wrath (my mother's *awesome* maiden name) and slunk back here to live out the rest of my life in what I thought would be a dull retirement.

It's been anything but. In the past year I've been framed for the murder of various terrorists and a prison escape by an American spy, fought off a smuggling ring at camp, and dodged the Yakuza in Washington DC, all with my troop of eight-year-old little girls in tow.

And I suspect they've loved every second of it. Kelly, my co-leader, wasn't so convinced.

Reverend Miller handed me Finn, and the little girl stopped crying immediately. As I looked into her tiny face, I thought she was smiling at me. And then I smelled it. My former career as a spy did not prepare me for this.

"Thank you everyone for joining us today," the good reverend said. Wow—I missed something. Was it over?

"Please join us in the basement for punch and cookies," he added.

I handed the baby to Riley. He was a natural with her. That's another thing I never knew about him. I watched as his grin faded to horror when he smelled what just happened.

"I'll change her, Riley." Kelly stepped up and took her daughter from my former boss's arms. "Head downstairs and we'll meet you in a moment."

"Nice of you to take time off from work for this," I said as the two of us descend into the dungeon of horrors.

"I wouldn't miss this for anything," Riley replied.

Huh. I didn't really expect that answer.

The church basement was actually not bad. My complete lack of experience in the churchy department had led me to believe it would be a torture chamber that would do the Spanish Inquisition proud. Instead, it was a sunny room with carpet and the Lutheran Ladies League standing behind a table full of cookies and bars. A large punch bowl filled with bright green liquid resembling antifreeze rested at the end.

Rex, my boyfriend and detective of Who's There's finest, was sitting with the twelve little girls from my troop. They were abnormally quiet. I wondered if he'd drugged them into submission.

"Thanks for watching them." I greeted Rex with a kiss.

"No problem. They've been great." He kissed me back. "I think they would've been fine up there."

I shook my head. "Kelly would never forgive me if they had a water war in the baptism whatchamacallit or swiped the wine and crackers."

An amused grin spread over my boyfriend's face. Oh sure, I knew those things had different names—I just didn't know what they were.

Before he could make fun of me, I asked, "How did you get them to be so quiet?"

Rex turned to look at the little girls. They were sitting completely still, wearing cute dresses and patent leather shoes. They looked expectantly at the doorway.

"I just told them if they were quiet, they'd get to hold the baby when she came down."

A unified scream that hasn't been heard since the war cries of Norse Berserkers in the twelfth century erupted from the table. Finn had arrived and was now surrounded by little girls reaching for her with sticky hands.

"You let them eat first?" I asked Rex.

He nodded. "I really had no choice."

I totally understood. But now the girls were sugared up and waging a greedy assault on Kelly. I turned away. She could handle it. I was thirsty, and even that neon green liquid in the punch bowl looked good.

"So, did you burst into flame when the reverend sprinkled you with holy water?" Rex asked as he ladled me a cup of the neon lime, frothy fluid.

I glared at him. "Why does everyone think that would happen? I'm an agnostic, not a Satanist, for crying out loud."

"That's a good thing," Kelly joined us, taking the cup meant for me. "Because we're having a Mommy and Me Movie Night lock-in here this weekend."

I stared at her. "What? Why?"

I'd managed to avoid doing a lock-in or any other kind of slumber party with our troop since our unfortunate trip to Washington, DC a few months ago. In fact, if I never shared a building overnight with my troop again, I'd be a happy woman.

"It's already arranged, and everyone is going. Including you." Kelly shot me a look before rescuing her husband Robert—who was still under siege by the girls.

Rex watched her go. "She's still mad at you."

I poured my own cup of punch and took a sip. Ooooh! It was good! I'd have to get the recipe from the Lutheran Ladies League before I left.

"Yes," I answered. "She still hasn't forgiven me for the whole Evelyn thingy."

Rex turned his eyes on me. "Really? She's still mad because you took an adult with you who wasn't a parent—no one even knew her—who disappeared the minute you got back?" He picked up a Rice Krispie bar and studied it. "I wonder why?"

I threw my hands up in the air. "I thought she was one of the Kaitlin's moms! She said she was a parent and volunteered to go! How could I possibly know she was some weird, mysterious Girl Scout groupie?"

"You're right. Kelly's so unreasonable," Rex laughed.

I grumbled as I poured another glass of punch, filled my plate with cookies, and stomped over to a table. Rex and Riley joined me. Rex was eating. Riley was not. He was a bit of a health nut, and I'd guess he drew the line at glow in the dark beverages.

"You still haven't found her for me," I accused.

Rex shook his head. "I've done as much as I can. But there's no Evelyn Trout in any database, anywhere."

"She exists," I insisted.

And I knew this because I'd spent a week in Washington, DC with her and my Girl Scout troop. Maria Gomez, my friend from the CIA, saw her too. She'd offered to help me locate the woman, but I'd felt like I already used up all my favors at the

Agency. Maria had put her job on the line to help me before, and I didn't want her to have to do it again.

"I believe you," Rex said, hand over his heart. "It's just weird that she isn't in any pictures from your trip."

That was weird. The girls had taken lots of pictures on the trip. I was in several—and they weren't very flattering, if you asked me. Why the girls thought they needed hundreds of close-ups of my nose, chin, and left eye was beyond me. Maria was even in some of the photos (and she looked fabulous in every damn one). But there wasn't even a *glimpse* of Evelyn Trout in any of them.

Who was this woman? And why did she go with us? Who in their right mind would tag along to Washington, DC in the heat of summer with a Scout troop? I wouldn't have—except that I'd had no choice.

I decided to ask Riley. That man owed me big. Like a rage virus King Kong fighting a zombie Godzilla big. And I wasn't going to let him off the hook.

The baby started crying, which signaled to me the end of this party. It wasn't fun anymore if the guest of honor was crying. That was true if you were a baby or despotic world leader. It was time to go.

Rex and I led my troop of girls outside where we waited until they got picked up one by one by their parents. I tried to remember each mom's name as she drove up. That would show Kelly. Then, there'd be absolutely no need for a lock-in. The plan was foolproof.

Okay, the spirit behind the plan was foolproof. Except for the fact that I didn't know a single mother who showed up. I decided we'd need nametags for the lock-in. And even then, I wasn't guaranteeing anything.

"Did they each get in the right car?" Kelly asked as her little family made an appearance outside. "With the right parent?"

I was not going to roll my eyes in front of Finn. That seemed disrespectful somehow. Did babies understand sarcasm?

Rex nodded. "I made sure of it."

"Thanks Rex," Kelly kissed him on the cheek. "At least one of you is responsible."

Finn started to cry again. I rolled my eyes. No reaction.

"Hey, I'm responsible! We made it through an entire trip without anyone dying."

Kelly just shot me a look before she and Robert and the baby (who had a deplorable lack of understanding of sarcasm) left.

"Shall we?" Rex held out his arm.

I nodded. "We shall."

We'd had the whole evening planned. Rex and I were going to cuddle up on his couch with my Hitler-resembling cat, Philby, and her three kittens. Rex had rented a couple of movies, and I was bringing the popcorn because that was the one snack the felines didn't like and therefore, didn't mess with. I'd learned the hard way that cats love cupcake frosting, bacon, and hamburgers. Philby liked to touch any meat you were eating with her paw. Then she'd sit back and wait for us to be grossed out. No cat should be that smart.

"It was nice seeing you again, Wrath." Riley stepped outside as he buttoned his suit jacket.

Rex held out his hand and Riley shook it. "Are you heading back to DC?"

Riley nodded. "Yes. I've got a lot of work to do."

I didn't ask him to help with the Evelyn search—it wasn't the right time or place. See? Responsible! I didn't even think about asking…okay, I thought about it. But I managed to control myself. Because…responsible!

"Do you need a ride to the airport?" Rex asked.

"No. I've got a rental car. But thanks." Riley gave me look I couldn't interpret before walking away.

Rex and I headed back to our houses, which were, conveniently, across the street from each other. After changing clothes, I filled a laundry basket with popcorn and cats and headed over.

"Just in time," Rex said with a smile as he opened the door.

"For what?"

Oh crap. Had I forgotten something? If Kelly was here, she'd shake her finger and tell me how irresponsible I was. Good thing she wasn't here. I stepped over the threshold and released the cats as Rex closed the door.

"For this," Rex said before taking me into his arms and kissing me.

Oh right. For that. I shouldn't be late for that.

Meeeeeooooooow! Philby protested loudly. We looked down to see her sitting there, like a feline Hitler who was angry with her generals.

Rex picked up the popcorn package and I followed him to the kitchen. I demonstrated my mad cooking skills by popping a bag in the microwave. Three minutes later, we were sitting on the couch, watching some long, historical film with lots of war stuff and men and women pining on the edges of cliffs.

Philby took her usual position between us. After a few minutes, she claimed Rex's lap and curled up, falling asleep. Her kittens, however, were going crazy. What was it about kittens that made them act like rip roaring amphetamine junkies? Two of the kittens, Moneypenny and Bond, were wrestling furiously with each other. I know—it's a cliché to use James Bond names for your pets when you're a spy. At least I didn't go with Pussy Galore.

The third kitten, a little girl who had a black Elvis pompadour, complete with sideburns, was racing back and forth across our laps with no goal in mind. Her name was Martini-Shaken-Not-Stirred. I called her Martini for short.

"Are you ready?" Rex asked halfway into the movie, interrupting my attempt at focusing.

Which was good because I had no idea what was going on. The plot was so twisted you'd need a crowbar to make it straight. And who puts like one hundred characters in a single movie? Madness!

"Um, sure." I was kind of hoping he'd meant *Ready to go up to my room?* Or *Ready for me to make a steak dinner?* Or even, *Ready to take a nap?* Any of those would've been good.

Rex laughed. I liked it when he laughed. "I meant ready for the lock-in?"

I grimaced. "No. I'm not ready. Hey! How about you go in my place?"

"No way. Besides, I think Kelly's right. You need to get to know the parents."

"Traitor," I said just before stuffing a handful of popcorn in my mouth.

"Maybe you'll get lucky," Rex said as he turned back to the TV.

"I doubt it," I mumbled.

"Could be worse," he said.

"How?"

"Your friend Juliette might show up." Rex ducked to avoid the pillow I'd thrown at his head.

Juliette Dowd was the only Girl Scout employee who hated me because I was dating her ex-boyfriend. Rex was right. I'd rather Evelyn Trout showed up.

Actually, I'd rather be chased by mutated Gila monsters across a burning desert. On Mars. While nursing a head cold.

But then, Juliette Dowd might be an improvement over an overnight lock-in with twelve little girls and their mothers.

CHAPTER TWO

───────

"Where do you want our stuff, Mrs. Wrath?" Inez asked me. She was holding the biggest sleeping bag I'd ever seen, two pillows, a blanket, and three stuffed animals. Was she planning on moving in here permanently?

"Over there, Inez." I pointed to the nursery on my right.

I'd showed up at the church an hour early for the lock-in so I could do some recon before the girls arrived. I didn't find any terrorists, secret tunnels, or members of the Illuminati. Which was good because I wasn't sure what I'd have done if I had.

Inez introduced me to her mother, Anna—a plump, short woman with long, black hair and eyes that seemed to smile. She nodded and nudged her daughter into the nursery and I turned to direct the next girl and her mom.

"What is this?" Kelly held up a wriggly Martini.

"That's a cat." I'd heard that having a baby strained your brain, but seriously?

Her eyes narrowed. "You brought the cats?"

I shrugged. "You brought a baby."

"It's not the same thing!"

Wow. She looked kind of mad. I took the kitten from her and deposited her into the arms of Lauren, who'd just showed up with her mother.

"The girls asked me to," I insisted, but I was lying. I just knew they'd love to see the cats.

"This is a church!" Kelly did that thing where she spoke quietly but was really about to lose it.

I nodded. "Duh. I know that."

Kelly threw up her arms and stomped away. I was in for it later. Philby rubbed up against my legs. She was a great cat, really. I'd thought she was a *he* when I'd adopted her. That's why I named her after the spy, Kim Philby. Of course, Riley reminded me constantly that Philby had been a spy for the Soviets during the Cold War. But I didn't like or want the cat at that time. Besides, I gave the kittens better names.

When Philby had showed up on my doorstep next to a dead guy, she was enormously fat. I didn't realize that she was pregnant—I just figured that mice were very, very fatty (of course back then, I thought that was all cats ate. I've since been proven wrong…repeatedly). But she was well-behaved, except for an unnatural interest in Rex. And she only had one quirk. She'd hiss whenever she heard the name…

"Bobbi!" Kelly called out as she came forward to hug Lauren's mom.

Philby hissed so hard she actually shot backwards. She went about three feet. Did they have Olympics for cats? Cuz that would be awesome.

"Oh!" Kelly slapped her hand over her mouth. "I forgot." She leaned in towards Bobbi and whispered loudly enough for me to hear (which really doesn't qualify as a whisper, now, does it?). "Sorry. Philby has an unfortunate reaction when she hears the name Bob."

Philby, who'd just managed to regain the three feet she'd lost earlier, hissed loudly again, this time falling over on her side. She stayed like that, probably in anticipation of hearing that name again, and decided that was safer.

"What a sweet kitty!" Bobbi knelt down and began to pet the cat.

"She has kittens too, Mommy!" Lauren giggled, pointing to Martini who was now asleep in her arms.

"How fun!" Bobbi stepped up to me, holding out her hand. "*I'm…*" She looked at Philby. "*Lauren's mom!*" she shouted at me.

"Oh, okay," I took her hand and shook it. "I'm Merry, Lauren's leader."

"*Nice to meet you!*" the woman shouted back.

Bobbi, or Lauren's Mom—as I'd decided to call her throughout the next twenty-four hours so my cat didn't fall into a hiss-induced coma—was tall and slender. She was immaculately dressed and like her daughter, had bright red hair.

"It's okay," I insisted. "You don't need to shout."

Bobbi looked confused, glancing from me to Kelly, "Oh…but I thought you said she was…"

Kelly interrupted, "You can put your gear in the nursery. Have you met my baby yet?" Wrapping an arm around the woman, she guided her to the room on my right.

"What was that all about?" I asked out loud.

"Mrs. Albers told my mom you're an imbecile," Lauren said matter-of-factly.

I decided that this was a teachable moment. "Imbecile doesn't mean deaf. It means, well, not very smart."

Lauren cocked her head. "So, you're stupid."

Well, I do have those days. "No. Mrs. Albers is clinically insane. That means crazy."

The child shrugged. "Okay."

With Martini still in her arms, she turned to follow the two women.

"Great," I mumbled.

I decided right then and there that when little Finn grew up, I was going to tell her some very interesting stories about her mother as a teenager sneaking out of her house in the middle of the night to go to parties. Maybe I'd even tell her what her mom did at those parties. That kind of made me feel better.

Only ten of the twelve girls showed up because Hannah and Emily were sick with the flu. Yes, that's sad, but yay! I didn't have to memorize two more names!

Kelly gathered everyone together in the gym, which included one baby and four cats. I was still stunned that this church had a gym and was just going to ask about it—but Kelly didn't seem to want to talk to me.

The gym itself was pretty cool. Kelly had thought we could play some games there. I'd been over the moon when I found a bunch of rubber balls. Uh-oh. Were we playing dodgeball later?

She held up her hand in the quiet sign, and the girls immediately responded by copying her.

"I ordered pizza!" Kelly said. Why was she saying I instead of we?

"It will be here any minute," she continued. "Mrs. Wrath—" Kelly used the title the girls always mistakenly called me, just to make me mad—"will go up to the vestibule right now to wait for the delivery."

The girls squealed, the sound bouncing around the gym, before Kelly held up her fingers in the quiet sign.

"We will watch movies after we eat. I've got all the Harry Potter movies!"

Another echoing squeal went up, and Kelly turned to look at me expectantly.

I glared at my best friend and stomped away. Fine. I'll pay for the pizzas. But she'll be sorry. And that's when I'd realized I had no idea what a vestibule was. Was it a doorway? If so, I'd found four separate entrances when I'd done my reconnaissance earlier. Which one was I supposed to meet the pizza guy at?

After ruling out an entrance by the kitchen and an entrance by the offices, I headed toward the main lobby—or at least what I thought was a lobby. The final entrance had been by the gym, but Kelly was so mad at me right now I'd figured she picked the door that was farthest away, just because.

I didn't know we were watching Harry Potter. I knew nothing about those movies. Was it about a werewolf who made ceramic stuff? I'd have to act like I knew what was going on. I was pretty good at that.

It was still light outside, and September still hadn't shed its late summer heat. I stepped outside, sat down on a bench, and waited. I was a little confused by Kelly's behavior because I was doing what she'd wanted. I was here at the lock-in, and once I went back inside I could get to know the mothers.

It really wasn't fair for her to be mad. She's the one who got pregnant and couldn't go with us to DC. *I* didn't get her pregnant…because…well, science. And what about her telling Lauren's mom that I was an imbecile? That didn't seem very mature or responsible to me.

Once this slumber party was over, I was going to devote every waking moment to finding out who Evelyn Trout was. I had some favors I could call in. And I knew a few things.

For instance, Evelyn had a Midwestern accent. Either she was an excellent mimic or she was from around here. Well, within a five-hundred-mile radius anyway. Also, the woman was middle-aged and had no sense of humor. I wasn't sure those two things were related—since I wasn't quite there yet.

Oh for crying out loud. This train of thought wasn't getting anywhere. My mind was too frazzled. If I was going to survive this sleepover, I'd need to focus on what I came here to do. As for Kelly and her rotten attitude? Well obviously it wasn't my fault. And I'd tell her that as soon as the pizza guy got here.

A crappy little car blasting death metal music screeched to a stop a few yards away. The teenager who got out looked completely bored as he pulled five, huge pizzas from the back seat. I waited until he walked over before standing up.

"You with the group here?" The kid's voice squeaked. He looked to be about seventeen, with oily hair and a weak chin.

"That's right," I said as he handed me the boxes.

"That'll be $125," he said, crossing his arms over his chest.

My jaw dropped. "You're joking."

The boy shook his head and stuck out his hand. "Cash or check is fine."

I glared at him, "That's like, twenty-five bucks per pizza! What are they made of? Caviar and truffles?"

He shrugged and stuck out his hand again. Clearly this conversation was beyond his pay grade. I didn't have $125 on me. I didn't even have my purse on me. What was Kelly thinking? There was a place up the road where you could get large pizzas for five dollars each!

The kid looked like he was going to call someone to come make me pay. I had no choice.

Very carefully, I set the pizzas down on the bench and pulled my cell out of my pocket.

"Rex?" I said the minute my boyfriend answered. "I need your help."

Rex handed the kid what looked like $130. A five-dollar tip? Seriously?

"That's for having to deal with you." Rex winked as the kid walked away.

I sighed. "Thanks for helping me out. I'll pay you back the minute this thing is over."

"It's okay. I know you're good for it." Rex kissed me, then walked back to his car and drove off. I was really lucky to have such a great boyfriend.

"What took you so long?" Kelly asked as I walked into the gym, carrying five possibly cold pizzas.

"I thought you'd paid for them already." I narrowed my eyes for an intimidating effect.

My best friend ignored it. "You didn't take your purse out with you?"

"Nope. And did you realize how expensive those things were?" I pointed at the boxes that had been scooped up by the moms.

Kelly laughed and nodded. "I did." She turned on her heel and walked away.

So that was it. She was going to get back at me with these little, passive-aggressive moments. Like telling the mothers I'm an imbecile. Like making me pay for the over-priced pizzas. Well, two could play at that game! I was gonna...

What? What was I going to do? Harass a woman who'd just had a baby? A baby she'd named after me? No. I'd have to just grin and bear it. And really rack up those scandalous stories to tell her daughter someday.

Everyone was sitting on the floor, munching pizza. Kelly had distributed juice boxes earlier. It was probably the quietest moment we'd ever had as a troop. A screen had been pulled down from the ceiling in my absence, and some weird projector was hooked up to a laptop. Kelly punched a few keys, and this weird little music came on. The movie was starting.

I grabbed a couple of slices of pepperoni and joined the four Kaitlins on the floor. The kittens were fascinated by the long strings of cheese that were connected to every slice. I giggled as I watched them swipe at the cheese, and the horrified looks on their faces when it stuck to their paws.

Were cats stupid or smart? I couldn't really get a read on that. Sometimes, they did things that I would've thought centuries of evolution had bred out of them. Other times, they looked at me as if I was the supreme idiot of the universe. It was mind boggling to say the least.

The movie started and I realized Harry Potter was some sort of boy wizard. It only took minutes to get swept up in the story. Wow. His family was horrible. If this kid was a wizard, I hoped he'd turn them into incontinent goats or tiny planarians.

The girls were transfixed. And I was right there with them. For two hours, I gobbled down pizza while I stared, hypnotized by the film. It was a good story. I liked the part about Diagon Alley. I'd love to have an owl like Hedwig. Of course, he probably wouldn't get along with the cats too well.

The movie finally ended, and I joined the girls in begging for the second film to start.

"Not until we clean up," Kelly insisted.

We ran around picking up, and I even volunteered to take the garbage out. I couldn't wait for the second movie. How did I not know about this series? You'd think Rex would've told me about Harry Potter. Right?

When I returned to the gym, the girls were setting a dozen rubber balls on the middle line.

"Dodgeball!" The girls seemed to cry out in unison.

Oh no. Not dodgeball. I wanted the second movie! I'd always hated the game when I'd been in school. Mostly because I was terrible at it. Seriously. I was so bad, that even with no one aiming at me, I usually was the first one out. At least it gave me some experience for being a spy. One time, in Africa, these monkeys were hurling fruit at me, and I didn't even get hit. Not even once.

But now? An idea slowly dawned on me. Now would be my redemption. How could I lose? First of all, I was bigger. And second, my hand-eye coordination was way better. For once in my life, I was going to win. Harry Potter could wait until I had my moment in the sun.

Kelly stepped up to the center line. Moms on one side, kids on the other. She blew a whistle, and we all raced toward those rubber balls. I got there before everyone else and managed to knock Betty and Lauren out with one throw. This was too easy! I quickly dispatched the rest of my troop and did a little end zone dance to celebrate my victory.

What I hadn't counted on was that an adult going after children by hurling rubber balls at them would come across as somewhat cruel. By the time the first round was over, ten little girls were crying in their mothers' arms. Their mothers were shooting death glares at me, which was odd since I was on their team.

Kelly blew her whistle and called me over to the sidelines. I danced my way over to her, still celebrating my dominance as Dodgeball Queen. Take that, junior high gym teacher, whose name I can't remember!

"Really?" Kelly had her hands on her hips.

"What?" I asked a little defensively.

"This is supposed to be fun." My friend shook her head. "You turned it into a bloodbath."

"I hardly think that qualifies as a bloodbath…" I grumbled. "There's no blood, really."

"Then," Kelly said through her teeth. "What do you call that?" She pointed to my right.

One of the Kaitlins had a huge, red circle on her arm. She gave me furious glances that said I should probably sleep with one eye open tonight.

"You might be a little, tiny bit right," I mumbled.

"I'm totally right, and you know it," Kelly fumed. "This is supposed to be fun. You are supposed to get to know the parents. Not body check them."

Oh. Right. I gave Betty's mom a sad shrug.

"Sorry, everyone. Really. I shouldn't have been so competitive."

Inez winked at Betty and whispered something. I thought I heard *wait until she's asleep.*

Maybe I shouldn't sleep at all tonight.

CHAPTER THREE

———

Kelly decided that as punishment for my rather aggressive dodgeball slaughter that I should lead the arts and crafts portion of the evening's activities.

"I don't know. I think we should watch the second movie before it's too late. I'd hate for the girls to go to bed without seeing what happens to Harry Potter next." I tapped my watch.

"I don't think you fully understand what a lock-in is." Kelly handed me a ream of construction paper that could be used to wallpaper the entire church.

"It's a sleepover." I made a face as I pulled glue sticks and safety scissors out of a box. Safety scissors. What a joke. I could still kill one, maybe two men with a pair of these.

Kelly shook her head. "Oh, there's no sleeping here tonight. It's an all-night party."

What? "What? You're kidding! I didn't sign up for that! I distinctly remember the words *lock-in*, not *stay-up-all-night-driving-your-leader-crazy*."

Kelly put down the pipe cleaners. I had no idea what kind of craft we were going to do, but it seemed terrifying.

"Look, Merry," she said. "I know you've kind of had issues about spending the night with the girls since you got back…"

I nodded. "Yes, and I think I told you I've used up a lifetime of sleepovers on that one trip." I really did say that. And she really wasn't amused. Kind of like now.

"You've been the leader of this troop for a year and a half. You've gone camping with them, taken them on a trip to Washington, DC, taught them how to build fires, and tie knots. What did you think it meant?"

I sighed. "You're right. I guess I'm still a little jumpy about the whole thing."

You might think that running a troop of little girls would be easy after having been a spy. You might think that something like this would be a piece of cake, especially since, as a rule, Girl Scouts aren't armed with automatic weapons. And maybe you might believe in unicorns that shoot lasers out of their butts.

Running a troop has been the best and worst thing that's happened to me since I retired. Actually, more best than worst. Probably 60/40. Or maybe 70/30. Never 80/20 though. That would be going too far.

The fact was, I loved these kids. And as weird as this is going to sound—I thought of them kind of like my family now. But if you ever told them that, I would hunt you down and torture you. Never give your enemy information they can use against you.

I grew up in Who's There, Iowa. When I went to college, my parents moved to Des Moines, and my dad launched his political career. Now an important senator in DC, Dad and Mom live there now.

When I was outed, I decided to disguise myself and come back here. Kelly was the only one who really knew me then. I was kind of a wallflower back in the day—to the point I was invisible. Now being back here as Merry Wrath instead of Finn Czrygy, I was still kind of invisible.

Which meant that I didn't really know anyone. Kelly talked me into being a co-leader for a troop. These girls became my family. My short, in some cases toothless, giggly, screamy family.

"I'll work on it," I promised Kelly.

"Yes you will," she answered before walking away.

"What? No hug?" I called out after her.

She just shook her head before she disappeared into the hallway.

Fine. I organized the craft materials into equal piles on each table. It had to be exactly equal, I've learned. Kids had radar for one getting more than another. And if one girl had one more sheet of yellow paper or one more pencil than the others, you would hear about it.

The girls and their mothers poured into the room and gathered around the tables. For a moment, I panicked because I had no idea what we were doing. I'd forgotten to ask Kelly. The girls turned quietly and expectantly toward me.

Meeooooooow!

Philby entered the room, trailed by Moneypenny, Bond, and Martini. It gave me an idea.

After placing an empty box on each table, I deposited a cat into the box. The one thing I have learned over the short time of my cat ownership is that cats love boxes. There are no exceptions to this. None.

The kittens enjoyed the attention, but Philby was dubious. I made sure to put her at a different table than Bobbi. I didn't even want to *think* her name, just in case my cat could read minds.

"The cats are your models," I announced. "Everyone— make a cat using the materials in front of you."

There! That seemed simple. I heard Finn crying down the hall. Kelly could handle the baby. I totally had this. And once we were done, we could watch the second movie. You know what? Maybe the staying up all night thing would work after all. I'd get to see at least two more movies in the series. Seemed like a win-win to me.

I made the rounds of the tables, replenishing supplies and introducing myself to the moms I hadn't really met yet. Although, when you play dodgeball together—you get to know people fairly quickly. Especially when you brain them with your elbow or knock their kid unconscious with a red rubber ball.

At the first table sat the four Kaitlins and their four mothers, all inexplicably named Ashley. To make things even more difficult, the women were all the same height, with brown hair and eyes like their daughters. It was as if these women and their daughters were all cloned from the same DNA and, for some reason, given the same names.

There was no way I was going to be able to tell these women apart. Even their features were nondescript. I know that seems like a strange description, but it was the truth. These women could fade into the woodwork and be completely forgettable. And while that was an admirable skill for any spy, it was a pain in the butt for a Girl Scout leader who was trying to get to know the mothers of her girls. For now, they'd just have to be known as the Ashleys—mothers of the Kaitlins.

The next table had Betty, Lauren, Inez, and their mothers. Including Lauren's mom—she-who-must-not-be-named (aka Bobbi). Betty's mother was named Carol Ann. She was a pretty woman with a blonde bob and perky smile.

"You must be Mrs. Wrath!" The woman jumped up with great glee and flung her arms around my neck. "Isn't this just the most fun ever? I can't wait to see what we do next!"

Oh yeah. Definitely perky. I was pretty sure I hated her. And what was up with the adults calling me Mrs.? It was bad enough that the girls did. But the adults should've known better.

Hannah and Emily were sick at home. But I still had the other Hannah, Caterina, and Ava's moms to meet. The good news was I'd never forget Lauren's mother's name, nor the four Ashleys. But Betty's perky mom and Inez's sweet mom's names were fading with every second.

"Hey!" I knelt down next to Ava. "How's it going?"

This was Philby's table. While her kittens were enjoying their new careers as models, Philby was sitting and glaring at the girls. She didn't mind them petting her, but I got the distinct feeling she felt a little objectified and was not happy about it. Still, not one of them had even attempted getting out of the box. Should we ever be invaded by an evil, feline horde, all we'd need to defeat them are empty boxes. Maybe I should start stockpiling them.

Caterina held out a bunch of rectangular pieces of different colored paper, all glued together in one spot. There were about fifteen pipe cleaners, all on one end.

"This is Philby!" She grinned through a huge gap in her teeth.

Some kids lost their two front teeth. Caterina lost six. At the same time. She'd told everyone that the tooth fairy had left her sixty bucks. Sixty! I think I got a quarter back in the day.

"Of course it is. And these are the whiskers." I said brightly, trying to focus on her sculpture.

Philby turned her glare on me. Some cats just didn't understand art.

"Hello." A woman about my height, with very curly brown hair and very large brown eyes extended her hand. "I'm Lola—Caterina's mom."

I took her hand and shook it, introducing myself. Ava's and Hannah's mothers introduced themselves—Megan as Ava's and Penny as Hannah's. I tried to find a way to remember them, but it was hopeless, because now I wanted nothing more than to get back to my Harry Potter addiction.

Names weren't originally a problem for me. In the field, I'd had no problem remembering people's names because they were either my mark, target, or colleague. My life kind of depended on remembering who was who.

"What are you doing?" Kelly appeared magically at my side. She had an annoying way of doing that.

"What do you mean?" I pointed to the cats on every table. "We're doing a craft. And the cats are the models."

Kelly looked around. "I was going to have them make pinwheels."

I stared at her, "Like the Easter things that spin around?" I looked at the supplies. "How did you think that was going to work exactly?"

Finn belched—which was adorable. Everything my namesake did was adorable. Everything.

"I guess." Kelly had a glazed look in her eyes. "That's fine. Good job."

She looked tired. Of course she was. The woman had a two-month old baby now. From what I understood, new moms didn't get much sleep, like ever. I couldn't possibly survive that. No matter how cute the baby was.

Maybe I should've cut her some slack. She wasn't sniping at me. It was her lack of sleep that made her irritable.

"Hey," I said, taking Finn from her. "Why don't you have your parents or Robert watch the baby tonight?"

It was like watching a person slowly go insane. Only instead of a person, it was Kelly. And instead of slowly, it was, like, one second.

She burst into tears, "You don't love my baby!" Kelly snatched Finn from my arms and ran from the room crying.

I looked around the room thinking that the moms would be like, *Wow. Crazy, right?* But no. Instead they looked at me as if I'd just tied up my own kittens with pipe cleaners and set fire to them.

I couldn't win. I really couldn't.

"Mrs. Wrath made Mrs. Albers cry!" Betty and Lauren weirdly yelled simultaneously, pointing at me like Donald Sutherland at the end of *Invasion of the Body Snatchers.*

"Single women!" I heard Ashley say to Penny as she shook her head slowly.

"I didn't…that wasn't…" I stumbled trying to explain myself, but it was useless. No matter what I said, this room full of mothers and their progeny wouldn't take it well from a woman who could barely handle a cat and three kittens.

"Women shouldn't judge other women." The perky Carol Ann glowered. Wow. She got dark in a hurry.

I looked around the room and sized things up. I was outnumbered. When faced with these odds, there was only one thing to do.

"Sorry," I apologized, adopting my most contrite look. "I'll go find Mrs. Albers and fix things."

I fled the room as if being chased by peasants with pitchforks and torches (which, by the way, they still do in certain Eastern Bloc countries). The church was dark and silent. Where was Kelly? Finn wasn't crying—which would be totally useful right now.

None of this was her fault. What was wrong with me that I couldn't behave here? All I had to do was keep people happy and learn a few names. But like typical me, I was fighting it every step of the way.

Kelly probably felt like she had to be my mother too. Honestly, when did I start acting like a surly teenager? That wasn't me. I was an adult. I was very good at adulting. I stuck my head in the nursery, which seemed like the perfect place to calm down a baby. But no, it was empty. I worked my way down the hallway, checking every room. They sure have a lot of rooms here. I thought people only came here on Sundays. I must've been wrong about that too.

"Kelly?" I called out as I hit the gym. The lights were on but it was, you guessed it, empty.

"Kelly," I shouted again as I left the gym and went toward the kitchen. "Hey! I'm sorry. You're not hiding from me, are you?"

Kelly wasn't in the kitchen either. I wound my way through to the room where we'd had the reception a few days before, finding no one. That left the main auditorium, or whatever they called that place where everyone sits to hear the minister talk.

"Kelly?" I said quietly as I stuck my head in.

The lights were dim, but I could make out someone sitting in the front pew. Maybe Finn was asleep. I walked over, trying to be quiet.

"Hey," I said, laying my hand on my best friend's shoulder.

She burst into tears, "I'm such a failure!" Finn slept in her mother's arms, ignoring the outburst—which was good since Kelly was a loud crier.

"What are you talking about?" I said as I sat down next to her.

Kelly wiped her eyes, but continued to cry. "I don't know what I'm doing! I can't keep Finn on a sleep schedule! And she only took about two ounces of formula!"

It was like she was speaking in tongues. I couldn't understand what she was talking about.

"I'm sure it's all fine." I put my arm around her. "You're a great mom."

"No, I'm not!" Kelly burst into sobs. "I'm doing everything wrong! Did you know that in the last two months, I've called the pediatrician seventeen times? Me! A nurse!"

Seventeen times did sound excessive, but I wasn't about to say so.

"That's totally normal!" I lied. Or maybe I was right. I'd had no experience here.

Kelly dried her eyes again and studied me. "Do you think so? Because Dr. Samuelson told me to get a grip and stop calling him."

I'd need to have a little "conversation" with Dr. Samuelson. One that involved thumbscrews.

I shrugged. "Well, what does he know?"

She burst into tears again. "Everything! He's a baby doctor!"

I didn't say anything for a few moments. I'd never seen Kelly in hysterics before. This was weird and completely out of my skill set. Kelly was always calm and in control. Who *was* this woman?

"Well…" I tried to think of something to say. "You're a new mother. You can't be expected to know it all. Cut yourself some slack."

Kelly blew her nose and handed the tissue to me. What the hell was I supposed to do with this? I got up and walked toward the altar. Surely there was some wastebasket up here. Right? Guess what. You'd be wrong. So, I walked to the back of the room and, finding a bin there, chucked it before returning up the aisle to Kelly.

"You're right," Kelly hiccupped. "This is probably just my hormones going haywire."

Post pregnancy hormones? That didn't sound good. I'd have to avoid that.

"Sorry I've been so hard on you," Kelly added. "The Evelyn Trout thing wasn't entirely your fault."

This was good! Now we were getting somewhere.

"I mean, I should've helped you plan the trip and attended those meetings where you went over everything. I'd have known that woman wasn't one of ours."

Great. Not quite what I'd expected. Oh well.

"Thanks," I said. "So, does this mean I can go home tonight?"

She laughed and shook her head. "Not a chance. I still think you need to get to know these parents. We've gotten lucky that none of them knew about the imposter."

"No one knew?" That seemed odd. "The girls didn't talk to their parents?"

Kelly shook her head. "I really don't think so. No one has called asking me to explain."

I stood and helped her to her feet. "Let's get back. Who knows what's happened since we left."

"The girls' mothers are there. I doubt that anything has gone wrong."

We walked in silence back to the room. I felt a little stupid when Kelly took a short cut through the basement, but acted as though I knew that was there. Poor Kelly. She was a mess. After the lock-in, I was going to do some research on this postpartum madness. It seemed to me I should be prepared for anything. I just hoped it wouldn't involve weapons of mass destruction.

We walked into the room and stopped, jaws gaping. I couldn't believe what I was seeing. All the supplies were put away and the tables were spotless. Nobody had bits of paper glued to them or pipe cleaners sticking out of their nostrils. It was almost as if we'd never been there.

Meeeeeooooooow!

Oops. Scratch that. Philby was at my feet, giving me a glare that, if she'd possessed the power of acid spit, would've killed me. The girls had apparently, decorated my cat. Philby's head was orbited by multi-colored pipe cleaners twisted in ways I wasn't sure were possible. Pipe cleaners twisted around her legs, body, and tail so that she looked like a wired up cat mummy or was heading out to Burning Man.

The three kittens trotted over, each decorated in pipe cleaners. Martini had one tied onto her tail that she was chasing in circles. Bond and Moneypenny were swatting at each others' décor.

I was just about to lecture the girls on what I'm sure Philby considered animal abuse when Kelly started to laugh. Okay—so it was worth it for that. The laughter was infectious, and soon all the non-feline critters in the room were shaking with giggles.

Philby was not amused. But since she couldn't remove the pipe cleaners, she just sat there, staring at me. Yeah, I was getting no sleep tonight.

Kelly had the girls pack up the supplies and then led us to the kitchen for a late night snack of cookies and milk. I kind of wished I'd smuggled in some vodka or something, but the church might've frowned on that. She did promise me we'd go back to the gym to watch the next movie. I just had to mingle with the parents one more time.

We all made small talk as we ate. And I learned a few things about the moms. For instance, perky Carol Ann turned out to be a strange woman, who claimed she'd been kidnapped by aliens who taught her how to play the bassoon. Penny and Megan spent an unusual and unhealthy amount of time together and have given each other kidneys (not sure how that's possible). The Ashleys actually seemed normal, but I couldn't remember a thing about them. It was as if my brain was on auto erase.

"Okay, girls!" Kelly called out. "Time for mani/pedis in the gym!" She gave me a glance and added, "While we watch the next movie!"

The mothers and daughters squealed and raced out of the room. One of the Ashleys took Finn with her so Kelly and I could clean up. That was nice of her.

"Wow," I said as I tossed an empty cookie box into the recycling bin. "We went through ten packages of Oreos."

"And a gallon of milk," Kelly added.

"Who's in charge of the mani/pedis?" I asked.

"Bobbi," Kelly said.

A loud hiss came from the doorway. I couldn't see Philby, but I could see spit flying up into the air. After a few seconds, the cat recovered and trotted over to me. I scooped her up.

"Where are your babies?" I asked her. She didn't respond.

"The Kaitlins took them with," Kelly answered as she scratched the cat's head. "They were talking about painting their claws pink."

Uh-oh.

"Well, we'd better…" I stopped. "Did you hear that?"

It sounded like a thump outside the door.

"Probably a raccoon trying to get into the trash," Kelly said, handing me a garbage bag. "Could be dangerous. You should take this out."

I looked at the bag. "Really?"

Kelly put her hand to her chest. "I'm the mother of a new baby. I can't go out there and risk leaving Finn as an orphan."

I took the bag. "Fine. I'll do it for her. Not for you. For Finn."

Philby walked ahead of me to the door. After sniffing, she arched her back and hissed.

"I think you're right about the raccoon," I said. I picked up Philby and handed her to Kelly before opening the door.

The body of a woman fell forward and face down on the floor in front of me. She didn't move.

"What the…?" Kelly gasped.

She immediately launched into nurse mode, dropping my cat and kneeling to feel for the woman's pulse. Kelly looked back at me and shook her head. I dropped the trash and helped Kelly turn her over so she could, presumably, start CPR.

The body flopped over onto its back—unseeing eyes staring at the ceiling.

Crap.

"She's been dead a while. Who is this?" Kelly stood up. She looked at the body and then at me. "You know her?"

I nodded. "Kelly, meet Evelyn Trout."

CHAPTER FOUR

───────

Rex showed up almost immediately with an officer I'd known and loathed in high school.

"Hello Kevin," I said. He ignored me like he always did. He had no idea who I was or why I knew his name, and he just didn't care.

"What is it with you?" Rex said as he put on a pair of latex gloves.

"Excuse me?" I asked.

"Dead people always seem to show up at your door." Rex checked Evelyn-the-Corpse for pockets.

"No purse either," I said. "I already looked."

Rex arched an eyebrow. "You messed with the crime scene?"

I shrugged. "I wanted to know who she really was."

My boyfriend looked at me like a parent exasperated with a toddler with learning disabilities. He looked at me like that a lot, actually.

"This is Evelyn Trout." I pointed at the dead woman.

The body did not respond. It was dressed in capri pants and a blouse, as if she was going to a barbecue instead of a date with murder at a Girl Scout lock-in. Huh. I wondered if playing dead would've worked for me.

"*This* is Evelyn?" Rex stared at the woman. "*The* Evelyn?"

I nodded. I was pretty sure I'd made that clear.

"So," he said. "That's why you looked for ID."

"She's not what I'd expected," Kelly said.

"What did you expect?" I frowned. I know I'd described the woman to her.

Kelly shrugged. "I don't know, really. Just not what I'd suspected."

Bobbi came into the room. "Hey, Kelly, we can't find the polish remover…" Her eyes bulged when she saw the body. "Is that…is she…?"

Damn. I'd forgotten to lock that door or do something to keep the kids from popping in.

Kelly put an arm around the woman and guided her back to the doorway. "Keep the girls in the gym, will you? And don't tell anyone yet." She stood there until she was sure the mom was gone.

Rex shook his head. "I'll need to interview everyone here."

"Oh no," I said a little too enthusiastically, "I guess we'll have to cancel the lock-in…" Then I could go home and have a movie marathon of my own.

Kelly glared at me. "Tell me you didn't plant this body here to get out of the sleepover!"

My jaw dropped. "Of course I didn't."

Was that her hormones talking? Besides, I've only planted a dead body once, in Tangiers. It wasn't found for a few days, and in the hot African sun, that wasn't a good thing. Did you know dead bodies can explode? I didn't.

I put on my most innocent face. "I was looking forward to the midnight *calling of the aliens* ritual with Carol Ann."

"Okay—I know you didn't do it. But you could act at least a little more upset if we have to call the whole thing off." Kelly folded her arms over her chest indicating this conversation was over.

Rex cleared his throat. "Ahem…now that we've cleared up that Merry didn't kill Evelyn and plant her here, we should move on with the investigation."

Philby was standing next to the body, sniffing. She put a paw on the dead woman's left eye, and then started walking around her, sniffing everything.

"I'd better go check on Finn." Kelly picked up Philby.

I watched as she walked out the door. "You don't really need to interview everyone, do you? Kelly and I were the only ones here."

Rex shook his head. "If anyone else had access to this room tonight, I need to talk to them."

Remembering that everyone had, in fact, been in this room just before we found the body, I could understand that.

"What about the girls?" I asked.

Rex nodded. "Them too. I'll interview them in pairs with their mothers, in another room. I'll show the parents a picture of Evelyn to see if anyone recognizes her." He took a picture of the woman with his phone.

"Do you think one of them knows who she is?" I stared at Evelyn. It had never occurred to me to find out if the parents knew her. My spycraft skills were seriously slipping.

"Until I'm done here, they're all suspects."

I thought about that for a moment. Were any of these women capable of murder? Seemed unlikely, but if so, my money was on Carol Ann.

"The girls didn't know who she really was," I said. "Remember? I told you they insisted they'd never seen her before."

"That only rules out the kids." Rex shook his head.

"You weren't really considering that one of my girls did it?" Because that would be kind of awesome—having a diminutive little assassin in my troop. Okay—that would be *all kinds* of awesome.

Rex was staring at me. I wondered what expression was on my face.

"Well, with the things your girls have been exposed to, I wouldn't rule it out." He looked very serious. But after a second he broke into a grin. "I'm joking."

"Uh, duh, I knew that." *Now.*

"Let's start with you," Rex said. "Tell me what happened here."

I told him about the cookies and milk. How we'd all been in this room.

"I moved from table to table, mixing with the parents," I admitted. "I didn't really pay attention to whether or not anyone was by the door."

"It was probably noisy and chaotic," Rex said.

I nodded. "As usual. Kids and cats were racing around the room. I'm pretty sure Kelly was holding the baby the whole time."

Was Kelly capable of holding Finn and murdering a woman and dumping her outside at the same time? The woman had mad skills, and she was hormonally crazy enough to do it. But I was pretty sure she'd been in the kitchen the whole time.

"I don't see any blood," I said. "She wasn't shot. We turned her over because Kelly wanted to revive her. There weren't any stab wounds or bullet holes."

Rex pulled the collar away from the woman's neck. "No ligature marks so she wasn't strangled." He studied her arms, "No bruising or defensive injuries."

"Poison? Maybe?" I asked, trying to be helpful.

Officer Kevin walked over, holding a glass of milk and a plate of cookies. At the mention of poison, the man looked at his plate before shrugging as he sat down at a table and proceeded to eat.

"It's possible," Rex said. "We'll know more when Dr. Body gets here."

"Dr. Body?" I asked. Was that some sort of code name?

"The new coroner." Rex grinned. "Her last name really is Body."

I tapped my chin. "Now I have a full set."

Rex's eyebrows went up.

"My eye doctor is Dr. Blink. My dentist is Dr. Toothacher. Now the coroner is Dr. Body. It's a complete set."

My boyfriend shook his head. "Never heard of anyone who collected doctors before."

I would've responded. Probably with something witty. Except that I was distracted as the most beautiful woman I'd ever seen walked into the room. She was Asian—my guess was Korean with a little Polynesian blend. Her long, silky black hair cascaded around her shoulders in perfect waves. Her plump, pink lips drew back over a dazzling smile. And she had a Cindy Crawford beauty mark just to the right of her mouth.

"Ah," Rex shook the woman's hand. "Dr. Soo Jin Body, this is Merry Wrath."

I was right. Soo Jin was a Korean name. I just didn't feel like celebrating because this woman was dazzling. And she worked with my boyfriend. I wasn't sure I liked that.

"Nice to meet you, Ms. Wrath." Dr. Body extended a slim, pale hand.

I shook it. "Likewise. So, you're new? Welcome to Iowa."

She nodded. "I just moved here from San Francisco." She put her hand on Rex's arm. "Rex has been so helpful. It's a wonderful town, but I'm used to a much larger city. There wasn't much in the way of real estate here. I don't know how I would've gotten my house if Rex hadn't helped me."

I narrowed my gaze at my boyfriend. "Yes. He's super helpful."

Oh…we were definitely talking about this later. If he blushed in the next few seconds, I might be breaking out the thumbscrews as well.

Rex flushed red. "I didn't do anything." He avoided my eyes. "One of the officers was moving away, and I suggested his place. That's all."

Dr. Body smiled at him, and I toyed with punching her in the face.

"So…the corpse…" I said, trying to take the woman's attention away from my boyfriend. "Tell us what killed her."

And then, I'll follow you home to see this house Rex helped you with. True, she hadn't done anything wrong. But I find it's helpful to be prepared. Just in case.

"Right." She knelt beside Evelyn's body and proceeded to examine the dead woman.

My eyes would've been on her, but I'd decided to watch Rex instead. If he was going to leave me for this woman—I wanted to know—because the venomous centipedes I'd have to order would come all the way from Vietnam. Maybe I should order them just in case…

"It looks like she's been dead about four hours." Dr. Body frowned at her watch as she got to her feet. "My guess is heart attack. But I won't know for certain until the autopsy is done."

"Thanks, Soo Jin." Rex smiled and winked.

He winked at her!

"Kevin." He turned to the dimwitted officer who was starting on his second plate of cookies. "Take the deceased out to the coroner's van."

Yeah, Kevin. And while you are out there, use that van to back over Dr. Body once or thirteen times, please.

Once the officer, the corpse, and the coroner were out of the room, I turned on Rex.

"Really? You winked at her?"

Rex laughed it off, but he was obviously blushing. "I didn't wink. Are you jealous?"

"Of course I am!" What was the point in denying it?

He shook his head. "You have nothing to worry about. I only have eyes for one woman who has lots of corpses around her."

"You mean me, right?" Yes, dead people seemed to swarm to me like flies. But I wanted to make sure he didn't mean the good doctor.

Rex nodded, but he didn't take me into his arms and kiss my fears away. Sure, I knew he was working, but still…

"And why is a medical examiner called a doctor, anyway?" I grumbled. "I mean, doctors make sick people better. A medical examiner just works with the dead. It's not like they can heal them or bring them back to life or anything."

My boyfriend ignored me. "Go and send the mothers in, please."

"Fine," I said. But he hadn't heard the last of this. Not by a long shot.

"Rex is ready," I said to Kelly once I found her in the gym with the others.

She was standing in the corner with the parents. The girls were sitting on sleeping bags and looking worriedly at their mothers. Kids always seem to know when something bad has happened. Although, if my girls knew there was a dead body on the premises, they would've been the first ones to bug Rex to see it.

"Go ahead," Kelly said to the women.

They moved in a cluster toward the door. When they'd cleared the gym, Kelly turned to the girls, while holding a sleeping Finn.

"We have permission to tell them what happened." Kelly nodded toward the kids.

"The moms said it was okay?" That was a surprise.

"Yes. And they don't want to call off the lock-in either."

I glared at her. "You are lying." What did I have to do to get out of this sleepover? Kill someone else? How many bodies would it take for Kelly to send us all home? If I found out—I'd have to write that down for future reference.

She shook her head. "No. They said as long as the body wasn't here anymore, it was okay. What did the coroner say?"

I decided not to tell her about Dr. Body and how she was intent on stealing my man.

"It could've been a heart attack. She doesn't know for sure."

Kelly walked over to the kids and sat down on Inez's sleeping bag. She set the baby in her lap.

"Girls, I have to tell you something." Kelly hesitated for a second. "Remember Mrs. Trout—the one who went to Washington, DC with you?"

Betty nodded. "You mean the spy in disguise?"

Kelly frowned. "The spy? No, she wasn't a spy."

I thought about interrupting. After all, technically speaking, we didn't know that she *wasn't* a spy. But I decided not to. The girls had finally found out about my past when we were in DC. I kind of wanted to keep that intel on the down low.

Lauren winked. "Oh, of course she wasn't." Her voice had that over-exaggerated tone usually reserved for sarcastic cartoon characters.

I chose to say nothing. I wanted to see how Kelly did with this.

"Well, she wasn't. She was just a normal woman who lived here…somewhere…"

Inez shrugged. "I've never seen her around." This prompted solemn *Me neither/I haven't* all around the group.

"You'll just have to take my word for it," Kelly demanded. She was getting a little fried around the edges.

The girls all looked at each other, communicating silently like mind-reading ninjas.

"If you say so," one of the Kaitlins said.

I could tell that the girls didn't believe Kelly. And I'm pretty sure she knew that.

"Anyway, Mrs. Trout had a heart attack," Kelly continued.

Caterina's eyes grew larger. "Is she dead?"

"Was it murder?" Hannah asked.

"Can we see the body?" Betty shouted eagerly. The others looked at her, then at me, nodding.

I was about to tell them that she was dead, and no, they couldn't see her, when Kelly spoke up.

"I'm sorry to say that she did die," Kelly announced. "The police are talking to your mothers right now and will want to talk to you afterwards."

"Wow!" Another Kaitlin shouted. "Do you think one of our moms did it? Cuz that would be awesome!"

The girls launched into a loud discussion of which mother was the murderer. My money was on Carol Ann, but several of them thought it was one of the Ashleys. Even the Kaitlins thought their mothers made good suspects.

Kelly looked horrified. Maybe she was concerned that one day, Finn would have no problem thinking that her mother may also be a murderer. It was probably also the absolute glee in the girls' voices as they discussed whether or not one of the Ashleys would "get the chair" for the murder.

I finally spoke up. "We don't know that she was murdered. That's what the police are here to find out. The coroner thinks it could be nothing—like a heart attack. So don't get your hopes up."

Kelly shot me a look. I shrugged. After all, the girls would be disappointed if it wasn't foul play. That wasn't *my* fault.

"Is Dr. Body the one doing the autopsy?" Inez asked. How did they know her? How did they know about autopsies?

I nodded. "Yes. How do you know about Dr. Body?" Okay—so maybe I was hoping for a little dirt or scandal here from a bunch of eight-year-olds. Sue me.

Lauren said, "She came to our school to talk about her job."

Well, *that* seems a little gruesome for elementary kids.

"You know," a third Kaitlin said, tapping her chin. "It could still be murder. There are poisons that create heart attacks."

"Yeah," Betty agreed. "There's cocaine or quinine."

Caterina nodded. "She could've eaten rhubarb or blood root."

Where were these girls when I was in the field? Kelly thought differently, as she covered the sleeping Finn's ears. I wonder what she thought a two-month-old would pick up from this conversation.

"Or," Hannah piped up, "she could've been stung by a stingray or jellyfish."

The fourth and final Kaitlin shook her head. "Don't be a moron. This is Iowa. We don't have an ocean for her to get stung in."

"What's a moron?" Betty asked. Really? They knew about toxic poisons but not what a moron was?

Lauren pointed at me. "It's an imbecile, a stupid person. Like Mrs. Wrath."

Hey!

"*Or*," Kelly yelled, which had a quieting effect on the girls, "she just had a normal, average, run-of-the-mill, garden-variety heart attack."

"Well, you're a nurse, aren't you?" Hannah asked. "What do you think?"

Kelly looked startled. On the one hand, she didn't want to talk about this…but on the other, she was probably flattered that they knew her occupation and wanted her opinion.

"Let's not get ahead of ourselves," Kelly said. "I can't tell you what killed her. We have to wait to see what the medical examiner…"

"Dr. Body…" Caterina interrupted.

"Yes. We have to wait to see what Dr. Body says." Kelly was starting to turn a little green.

The girls once again launched into a lively discussion over whose mother killed Evelyn Trout. I probably should've proven my level of responsibility and stopped them, but I found the whole thing fascinating. I never would've accused my mother of murder. And certainly not with so much glee.

Officer Kevin appeared in the doorway. "Okay girls. Come with me." He had smeared Oreo crème filling on the left breast pocket of his uniform, and his lips were black with cookie crumbs. How much of our food had he eaten? And did he think we wouldn't notice?

We followed him down to the nursery where each girl was united with her potentially murderous mother. Kevin took the first duo—Lauren and her mother, Bobbi—away first.

Philby and her kittens were asleep in the corner on a large pillow. At least I didn't have to worry about *them* killing anyone.

Kelly followed the direction of my gaze. "Hey, I meant to tell you, don't forget to take your litter box home tomorrow when you go."

Litter box? Uh-oh.

"I will," I lied as I promised to take home something I hadn't brought. There had to be something somewhere in the church I could use.

"Don't worry—I'll take care of it," I repeated.

And somehow, I would.

CHAPTER FIVE

————

When everyone had been interviewed, Rex sent Kevin for me. I could've pointed out that the man had a milk mustache, but decided not to.

"How did it go?" I asked Rex once we arrived in the kitchen.

"Well, in spite of an alarming and universal belief that Ashley Maitlin killed our victim, I don't have anything." He snapped his notebook shut.

Maitlin! I had no idea which of the four Ashleys that was, but at least now I knew a last name.

"Any word from the coroner?" I asked, avoiding saying the stunningly gorgeous doctor's name. No point in reminding my boyfriend of this woman's assets.

He shook his head. "Not yet. It'll be a day or so. We don't move as quickly as they do on television."

I folded my arms over my chest. "Why not? Evelyn has to be the only body in the morgue. You'd think a *professional* could identify the cause of murder faster than that."

Rex rolled his eyes. "It's Soo's job. Not mine. And not my business on how fast she does it."

I sighed. "What do you think?"

"Well, I certainly have had a lot of suggestions from your troop. From poisonous plants to a tiny blue-ringed octopus found only near Australia, there are quite a few theories on what could've induced the dead woman's heart attack—if that's what she had."

He looked tired. "You should go home and get some sleep," I said as I put my arms around him.

Rex smiled. "Thanks for thinking of me."

"Of course!" I kissed him briefly. It was lovely. "And when you get home, could you bring over that spare kitty litter box?"

Rex gave me a look. "You forgot that?"

"Maybe…and text me when you get here so I can sneak it in without Kelly noticing."

"What have the cats been using this whole time?" Rex asked.

I shrugged. "No idea." I wasn't sure I wanted to know.

After one more kiss, Rex left, promising to bring back the litter box and stash it in the kitchen. That way I wouldn't have to leave under suspicious circumstances.

I rejoined my fellow lock-in attendees in the gym, where things were quieting down. Kelly had dimmed the lights, turned on the second movie (yay!), and Finn was asleep in her car seat. I scooped up the cats, telling Kelly I had to feed them, then met Rex already in the process of covert litter box activity. After showing the cats where they were supposed to go and saying good night to my boyfriend once more, I carried the animals back to the gym.

Everyone was laid out on sleeping bags, their eyes glued to the screen. I made my way to my sleeping bag and, fully clothed, lay down to enjoy the movie and immediately fell asleep.

"She looks awesome!" a little girl said in what seemed to be the immediate vicinity.

I was too tired to open my eyes and too afraid to find out what they were talking about.

"Do you think she'll like it?" another familiar voice asked.

"Who wouldn't like pink hair?"

I sat straight up, eyes open, to find myself surrounded by my troop. I smelled something chemical-ish, and my forehead felt wet. The girls laughed as I grabbed my cell phone, turned the camera to face me, and looked.

I had pink hair. Really pink. Like punk rock pink.

"What did you do?" I asked the girls as I got to my feet.

Lauren grinned. "We thought you'd like it."

"It's only your bangs," Betty said.

But I wasn't listening. Instead, I was running for the bathroom, where I stuck my head under the faucet and rinsed frantically. Rivers of neon pink poured off my forehead and circled the drain. When the water finally ran clear, I stood up and looked in the mirror.

Nope. I still had pink bangs.

"Whoa!" Kelly walked in the door, stopping dead in her tracks when she saw me.

"You know..." She stepped forward, cocking her head to one side. "It kind of works on you."

I just opened and closed my mouth. Like a fish. Then I looked into the mirror again. I'd be angry, but it didn't look too bad. Instead, it looked edgy—like the kids in that techno bar I was staking out in Berlin once.

"Yes," Kelly said, nodding. "It definitely suits you."

There were two ways I could go with this. I could freak out and throw a huge fit, promising to get even with a bunch of little kids. Or, I could embrace it.

"I don't think the girls were doing it maliciously," Kelly said.

"Are you sure about that?" I asked as I stepped closer to the mirror.

"It's kind of a professional job, too," my best friend murmured. "I mean, they didn't get any on your skin or clothes."

That's why Kelly was my best friend. The woman could talk me down from any disaster. Like my hair. Right now.

"Okay," I said.

"Okay?"

I nodded. "I guess I had it coming by falling asleep without a guard posted. On the other hand, maybe they thought they were doing something nice."

Kelly hugged me, and together we walked back to the gym. The girls looked worried, their eyes darting around in fear. They wanted to know what I thought. They really hadn't meant anything by it.

"I love it," I said with a grin.

The girls tackled me in a huge group hug just as the moms were starting to wake up. I hugged them back. After all, it could've been worse.

"So where's the rest of the dye?" I asked. "We should dispose of it before it stains something important."

The girls were all staring at me. Something was off.

"What is it?" I asked, kneeling down to their level. "Did you get it on a carpet? A chair?"

That wouldn't be good. I'd have to replace whatever it was before we all went home this morning. And I knew nothing about getting stains out of anything.

The girls began to part before me, making a path. I looked at them, trying to read the situation, but I couldn't.

Meeeeooooooooow!

The last two girls stepped aside. And sitting there, wreathed in feline fury, was my cat. A cat who was now bright pink. She looked at me like she wanted to strangle me in my sleep. Kelly gasped loudly, and the mothers came running over.

"The kittens?" I barely managed. I couldn't take my eyes off of Philby.

Lauren shook her head. "We didn't have enough dye for them too."

The other girls lowered their heads as if they'd failed by not turning the three kittens a vibrant pink. Astonishingly, there were no stains on the gym floor, but I did notice that one of Finn's baby blankets—the yellow one I'd given her—was completely pink.

The damp cat trotted over to me. I picked her up with a sigh and carried her off to the bathroom to be rinsed off.

She didn't like that, either. I used my sleeping bag to dry off the irritated feline. Philby looked at me for a long moment before running out of the bathroom. I followed her out into the hall to hear the girls cheering. One by one, they walked out of the gym, their bags packed, whooping it up. The mothers did not return my gaze. I noticed that none of *them* had pink hair.

"Mrs. Wrath?" Caterina tugged on my shirt.

"What is it?" I tried to keep my voice light and happy. It wasn't easy.

"*This was the best movie night sleepover ever*!" the child screamed before running down the hall to the lobby.

So, all it took to make these kids happy was cold pizza, a dead body, and a bright pink cat. I'd have to remember that in the future. Mainly so I could check their bags for contraband before letting them in.

If I ever agreed to do this again.

Rex came over a few minutes later to help clean up. He grinned when he saw my pink hair. But he laughed hysterically when he saw my pink cat. Philby gave him an icy stare. She didn't seem to be in a forgiving mood.

The kittens trotted up to my boyfriend and allowed him to pick them up. They purred like little tramps as he scratched their ears. After ten minutes of hauling stuff out to his car and double checking the church for any surprises left behind by the girls (or cats), I climbed into the passenger seat and closed the door.

"I like it," was the first thing he'd said to me since he'd shown up. "Why didn't you tell me you were going to do that?"

"Because I didn't know myself until I woke up like this," I said wearily.

It was about nine in the morning, and I was already exhausted and still wearing the clothes I had on yesterday.

"I love your troop," Rex muttered with a grin as he started his car.

Yeah, I thought. *Me too.*

"Any news on Evelyn's death?" I'd decided to change the subject.

Rex shook his head, "Nothing yet. Soo is starting the autopsy today, and Kevin is running her fingerprints through the system."

Kevin had the ability to run anything through any system? If I wasn't so tired, I'd demand to see it in person. But it was something else Rex said that bothered me.

I glared at him, "Do you always call her 'Soo'?"

"Of course. What would you like me to call her?" Rex seemed amused.

Personally, I'd prefer *Someone-I-Work-With-Who-I'm-Not-In-Any-Way-Attracted-To*. But I was pretty sure that wasn't going to happen.

"How about 'Doctor'?" I asked. "It is her official title, isn't it?"

Rex nodded. "Yes, but you of all people know how informal things are in a small town."

"Well maybe it should be more formal. Maybe you should call her 'Doctor' out of respect for her profession."

Rex didn't miss a beat. "In that case, you should always refer to me as 'Detective' when I'm working, and Kevin as 'Officer.'"

"Alright. I'll call you that in public. But Kevin will always be Kevin. Tacking a title onto a lobotomized goat doesn't change the fact that it's a lobotomized goat."

Rex slanted his eyes at me. "What is it with you and him?"

"I knew him in high school," I shuddered. "He was kind of our village bully, then our village idiot, and not much has changed."

Kevin had distinguished himself in one way back when we were in school—the man could eat anything (and I mean anything—I once watched him eat a live cricket). There was a much longer list of things he couldn't do…such as get any grade over a C-…or breathe through his nose.

"Has he complained?" I asked.

Rex shook his head, "No. I'd just like you to respect my colleagues."

"Fine," I sighed. It was not going to be easy, but for him, I'd try very hard to think about maybe honoring his wishes.

"So how come you never mentioned Dr. Body before?"

Rex frowned. "I'm sure I did. I must have."

I disagreed. "Nope. I'm pretty sure I'd remember a name like that."

We pulled into my driveway, and my boyfriend shrugged. "Huh. Thought I did."

"It's just that she made it look like you two have been working together for a while. You helped her find a house. That requires spending time together outside of work…"

"I'm sorry I never mentioned her before." He leaned across and kissed me. "It really must've slipped my mind."

I'll bet it did.

"That's okay," I lied. "Are you coming inside?"

"I'll help you get the cats inside, but I should head down to the office to see if anything turned up on those fingerprints."

Hmmm…Rex didn't usually go in on the weekends. And he'd said Dr. Body would be working on the autopsy today…

"Give me a call if you hear anything," I said as we walked up to the front door. I was soooo going to text him one hundred times.

Rex came inside and pulled me into his arms. "I will." He kissed me. "I promise."

I closed the door to see the cats staring at me. So, I led the four beasties to the kitchen where I opened a can of cat food. Philby momentarily forgave me when presented with the tuna blend—her personal favorite. The kittens greedily devoured the rest.

I took a long, hot shower. I might've shampooed and conditioned my hair thirty or forty times, and although I saw a little color circling the drain, my bangs were still extremely pink when I got out.

My short, dark blonde, curly hair was impossible. Maybe that's because I never blow dried it. Today was an exception as, armed with a round brush, I dried the hair with an ancient machine that I'd found at Goodwill.

A smooth bob was my reward, and while I kind of liked the new look, the bangs were still alarming. I guess there was nothing I could do about that. Meanwhile, Philby had decided to do her own bathing in the kitchen with no success. She looked like a huge, Hitler shaped lump of bubblegum. But I decided not to tell her that.

After a quick lunch of Pizza Rolls and ranch dressing, I sat down in the living room with my laptop and started googling every possible combination of Evelyn Trout that I could imagine. I'd already done this several times since returning from DC and had never found anything before. But hope springs eternal, and I'd decided to give it one more shot.

Nothing. There had never been a person on this earth who was named Evelyn Trout. I closed up my laptop and was just about to get a box of Girl Scout Cookies when my cell rang.

"Hey, Maria."

Maria Gomez was a close friend of mine back when we were both recruits at the CIA. She still worked there, and I'd just seen her a couple of months before on the DC trip. Maria was also my cookie pimp, blackmailing others at Langley (CIA HQ) into buying an insane amount of Girl Scout Cookies. In a word, she was awesome.

"Merry," Maria said, "what the hell happened out there?"

"Um…" I scoured my brain trying to come up with an answer. "I had a movie night sleepover with my girls…Kelly called it a lock-in."

"Really? I loved those when I was a kid," my friend gushed. But then her tone turned serious. "But that's not what I meant. Our system is lighting up over a fingerprint your boyfriend is running."

"You'll laugh," I said. "But those prints are from Evelyn Trout."

I explained the inconvenient appearance of the mystery woman. Maria had helped out on the DC trip, and she knew (or thought she knew) Evelyn.

"You're joking," she said in a voice that told me this was bad.

"I'm not."

You know that squishy feeling you get in your stomach when you know something is wrong? I had that. I didn't like it. If Evelyn's prints were showing up at the CIA, it wasn't good news.

"Well, then I sort of know who she was," Maria said. "Because Evelyn was a spy."

I groaned. "Crap."

I'd had terrible luck with dead spies and terrorists in the last year and a half here in Iowa. More than I'd had in all my years at The Company.

"Who did she work for?" I asked. "Her accent was flawless. Whoever she was, she'd done a good job of covering up her real identity."

"You have no idea," Maria said.

"What's that supposed to mean?"

"Well, Evelyn was a spy. But she wasn't from any other agency."

I gasped, "You don't mean…"

I could hear her nodding on the other side. "That's right. Evelyn didn't work for any other agency because…"

I finished her sentence for her. "Because, she's one of ours."

Evelyn Trout was CIA.

CHAPTER SIX

―――――

"How is this possible?" I asked, almost forgetting that Maria was on the other end of the line.

"I have no idea."

"You'd never seen her before when we were in DC?" It was a stupid question, I'll admit. If Maria knew who Evelyn was, she would've told me.

"Never. Remember, we don't know everyone in the Agency. It's not like we have a yearbook or anything."

I rubbed my tired eyes. "Okay…so who is she really, then?"

"I can't tell you that," Maria answered.

"Seriously? You're going to go all classified on this? With me?"

"No, you misunderstand," Maria said. "I have no idea who she is. That information is above my security clearance."

Maria was pretty high up on the totem pole at Langley. Yes, she jockeyed a desk now, but there wasn't much she didn't know or couldn't find out.

"I'm just calling to give you a heads up," Maria said. "The CIA is going to block the inquiry Rex submitted on her fingerprints."

That meant that Evelyn Trout was a big time Spook. That wasn't good. Not at all.

There were about a thousand more questions I wanted to ask Maria, but I knew she couldn't answer them. Besides, she'd get in trouble just for calling me with the heads up.

"Thanks for letting me know," I said at last.

"Don't pursue this any further, Merry," Maria warned. "You know that if her identity is locked down like this, you'll get attention you neither want or need."

"I understand. Thanks for calling." I ended the call and dropped back onto the couch.

Evelyn was classified. She worked for the CIA. That meant she was either disavowed for some reason, or she was Black Ops, or she was something I had no idea even existed. That would be just like Langley—to come up with something so bizarre no one else would think of it. At any rate, none of these options was good.

And being one of those things didn't explain why she'd been attached to our troop trip to Washington DC. It just made no sense. The woman had come all the way here, impersonated one of the mothers, and tagged along. Why would she do that? Why would anyone do that? Unless you're a deranged former troop leader who desperately missed traveling with kids, and the odds on that probably are nil, there's no reason to go with us.

My mind was spinning. What was I going to tell Rex? I had a sneaking suspicion that he wouldn't be satisfied with this explanation. And I couldn't tell him the intel came from Maria, because that phone call we'd just had never happened. Well, it did happen, but in the espionage ether, it didn't.

I had to shut this case down and do it now. If Rex asked too many questions, he could get into some serious trouble. The CIA would consider a detective from Who's There, Iowa to be nothing more than an irritating fly that needed to be swatted. There was no way I was going to let them do anything to my boyfriend.

Okay genius, how was I going to manage that? Maybe I should do nothing? In these cases, the Agency usually just placed a call or worse, came in person to end all inquiries. I wasn't sure Rex would agree with that. Because of my misadventures, he didn't really care about poking the CIA.

Ugh. This was worse than Evelyn being a stalker or weirdo. Which still begged the question—what was she doing hanging with us? Had the Agency assigned her to watch me? I wasn't a problem. Okay, so maybe I was, but I was trying to change my ways.

That had to be it. They were after me, somehow. It certainly wasn't the girls. Even with my troop, children weren't usually on a watch list. And aside from dying my cat pink, these kids weren't a threat to anyone but me.

I closed my eyes and leaned my head against the sofa. I definitely had to shut this down.

But then, I wouldn't know who she was and why she'd been on the trip with us. While I consider myself to be pretty good at self-control, my curiosity was screaming at me to find out what was really going on.

What do I tell Rex? Do I even give him a heads up? Maybe I should just let the Agency cut him off. That was probably the most prudent thing to do.

But then I'd be lying to my boyfriend. Okay, maybe not lying exactly, but keeping the truth from him. Rex wouldn't like that if he ever found out. And quite frankly, I didn't want to hide the truth from him. And if I lied to him, he might dump me. And when he dumped me, he'd probably cry on the shoulder of a certain knockout coroner and they'd start dating, get married, have children, and be happy ever after.

I kind of felt like I wanted to punch Riley in the throat right now. If he knew about this and didn't tell me...

Riley was a little higher up in the CIA than Maria was. Not by much, but maybe enough to discreetly inquire about Evelyn. Besides, he owed me one. Big time. Calling in that marker wouldn't be hard to do. And after he filled me in, I'd tell Rex and just have to insist that he didn't pursue it any further. That could work, right?

My cell went off again, and I picked it up.

"Merry," Rex said. It made me sad, because I liked his voice, and if I never heard it again it would be awful.

"What's up?" I tried to sound cheerful.

"Soo Ji...Dr. Body," he corrected. I loved him for that. "She found something. Evelyn had traces of acrylamide in her system. The coroner thinks the poison triggered a heart attack."

"So, she was murdered," I said.

"Looks like it," Rex replied.

"How did she find out so fast? Doesn't an autopsy take a while?"

"There was red, peeling skin on her feet and a little on her hands. It's a dead giveaway. The toxicology report won't be in for a couple of weeks, but she's seen it before."

"So it's not an official cause of death," I said.

"No. You can't tell anyone else about this until we know for sure," Rex insisted. I imagined him running his fingers through his short dark hair. He looked adorable when he did that.

"I just thought you'd want to know," he said finally.

Awww! He was thinking of me.

"Thanks," I said. "Any word back on those fingerprints?"

"Nothing yet, but it's the weekend. I figure it will be a while before we know on that account too."

Oh good. He was stonewalled. I wouldn't have to tell him anything right now.

"I'm going to be here late tonight, but how about ordering a pizza tomorrow?" Rex sounded hopeful, which was all kinds of awesome. I'm still amazed that a man like him wants a weirdo like me.

"Sounds great," I responded. We said our goodbyes and hung up.

That at least bought me a little time. Rex wouldn't get the cease and desist from the Agency for a few days. Maybe I could do a little digging before then.

My cell rang again. I was certainly popular today. The number was unfamiliar to me.

"Hello?" I asked. I never gave my name when I answered. Once a spy, always a spy.

"Mrs. Wrath. It's Lauren's mom."

"Oh, hello Bo..." I froze and looked at Philby, who'd just come into the room and was staring at me, waiting for me to say it.

Philby didn't like the name Bob. Every time she heard it, she hissed violently. Somehow, I thought she knew what I was about to say. She was preparing her spit for a massive blowout. We sized each other up, trying to decide who would give. It was the weirdest game of chicken I've ever played.

"Is everything alright?" I changed tactics, congratulating myself for outsmarting a cat.

"Everything is fine," the woman answered. "I just found something in Lauren's backpack that probably belongs to one of the other mothers. The girls were just stuffing whatever they found into their bags. She obviously picked it up by mistake."

This happened all the time. All. The. Time. Nobody ever took home only their own stuff. Usually it was an episode of Sherlock Holmes just to figure out who belonged to what. The worst was dirty underwear. No one ever claimed the underwear. At first, Kelly would wash the panties, but that changed nothing, and we just threw them away. We averaged about six pair of panties each overnight trip. Seventeen after we came back from DC.

"Okay," I said. "She can bring it to the meeting on Wednesday."

"Oh," Bobbi replied. "I think you should probably get it now."

Okay, why not? Running by and picking whatever it was up would be a welcome distraction. I wrote down the address and hung up. My keys were on the counter, and I snagged them. In seconds, I was in my car heading toward Lauren's house. I blasted the radio to scramble my thoughts so I wouldn't obsess about Evelyn Trout, and ten minutes later, I pulled into the driveway of a nice, middle-class split-level house.

People outside stopped working in their yards and stared at me. Way to make an entrance, Wrath. It must be the neon pink bangs. It didn't look like this neighborhood saw that very often. They probably had their pitchforks ready in case I turned out to be a witch.

"Hello!" I shouted brightly, adding a wave that made me look ridiculous. I made my way up the steps to the front door and rang the bell.

Lauren answered, along with the biggest dog I've ever seen.

"Hi, Mrs. Wrath! This is Clancy!" The girl opened the door, and I stepped inside.

Clancy looked at me before sniffing my legs. I haven't had much experience with dogs. Not much with cats either, but I was starting to consider myself an expert. After Clancy decided I was not a threat, he wagged his tail and climbed me like Mount

Everest. The dog stood on his hind legs, his front paws on my shoulders, his face looking down into mine.

I froze. Was this dangerous, or was I supposed to dance with him? Was that even a thing? And if so, did the dog prefer the tango or rumba? How was I supposed to know this stuff? Clancy responded by licking my face. It was like being mopped by a large, wet bath towel.

"Clancy!" Bobbi appeared and admonished the dog. "Down!"

The beast let himself down and looked dejected as he took the stairs to the basement.

"Sorry about that," Bobbie apologized. "He's rather friendly…"

"No problem," I said as I wiped drool from my shoulders.

The house was a typical split-level foyer. Just steps inside the house, you were confronted with the decision to go upstairs or down, as if the entryway was schizophrenic and couldn't make up its mind what level it wanted to be part of. Lauren and her mother opted for up, so I followed them.

We walked into the living room, and I stopped in my tracks. Bobbi apparently had an obsession with snails. The walls were covered with shelves and cases, each displaying snail sculptures. There had to be hundreds…maybe thousands of slugs in every shape, size, and color.

"You noticed my collection!" Bobbi clapped her hands together gleefully.

How could I *not* notice thousands (I'd decided that was the number) of slugs on the walls in every form imaginable? I kind of wondered if she kept the live version in her basement.

"I did." I nodded. "This is quite a collection."

The woman smiled so widely I could see all of the teeth in her head—which was totally disturbing.

"I have the largest snail collection in North America—the second largest in the world!"

"That's impressive." That's a thing? "How did you find out yours was the second largest in the world?"

Yes, I really wanted to know. What?

"Well, according to *Collectibles Weekly*," Bobbi was super excited now and started rocking back and forth. "They did a study and found out that a collector in Japan has more than me. But I definitely came in second."

Japan. That made sense. When I'd been stationed there, I'd seen some pretty weird stuff in people's homes. There's a magazine called *Collectibles Weekly*? And it's something that needs to come out every week?

"Wow. Maybe we could have one of our meetings here sometime, and you can talk to the girls about it." I was pretty sure there was a badge on collecting stuff. Plus—it would get me out of planning a meeting, so yay!

"I'd love to!" Bobbi squealed. She actually squealed. I made a mental note to wear ear plugs during the snail meeting.

"So…" It was time to get back to the reason I was here. "You have something that isn't Lauren's?"

"Oh yes! I almost forgot! Seriously—I could talk about snails all day long."

Yet one more reason to get out of here.

Bobbi pointed to the dining room table. Sitting in the middle of a field of snail printed placemats was a box the size of a deck of cards. I picked it up. It was made of dark wood, and there were some strange carvings on it—kind of a cross between hieroglyphs and runes.

"Have you ever seen that before?" I asked Lauren. Maybe she knew who it belonged to.

The little girl shook her head. "No. I'd remember something like this."

"Okay," I said. "I'll bring it to our next meeting. Someone must've left it behind."

I saw myself out in order to avoid seeing whatever was in the basement. I pictured a kind of snail hell—a slug version of purgatory—with Clancy as its Cerberus. And I didn't need to see that.

I was home in minutes. Philby was not in the living room, but three kittens were about three quarters of the way up my curtains. They cried, seemingly stuck there. I guessed that Philby got tired of their whining and fled.

"That's the eight millionth time this week!" I scolded as one by one, I detached the kittens from the drapes and plunked them on the couch.

The three kittens responded by piling on top of each other and immediately falling asleep. They were kind of narcoleptic that way. One glance at the drapes told me I had to do something about it. My curtains were starting to look like Swiss cheese. Maybe I should consider having the kittens declawed. Philby was fine—she never so much as scratched me. But her children…

I sat down beside the beasties and turned my attention to the box. It was missing a seam and hinge—in fact it was missing a way to open it all together. Shaking the box produced a rattling noise. Something was in there. Which meant a person (or after seeing Lauren's house—a snail) had put something inside. I wondered what it was.

It seemed like a weird thing for one of the girls to take to the retreat, and I hoped it didn't belong to the church. Maybe it was like that old Rubik's Cube—or whatever puzzle the kids play with these days. That seemed like a good answer. Well, if they can do it, I can do it, right?

For the better part of an hour, I worked on the box. After a few minutes I'd come to the conclusion that this was a puzzle box. Which sucked because I wasn't any good at puzzles. That didn't stop me, however, from wasting part of a day trying to figure it out.

Finally, I pulled out my cell and took a picture of the carvings. Maybe there was something about them online. That would be nice. Since I've had a smart phone, I've been able to answer the great philosophical questions. Such as, who sings that song from that movie we saw? Or why do Mexican jumping beans jump? By the way, I know the answer. The beans have little larvae inside who are trying to get out. The song thing I never did figure out.

I was just about to toss my phone on the coffee table when it buzzed.

"Riley," I answered. "Did you make it back to DC okay?"

"No," was my former handler's answer. "Because something came up."

"So where are you?" I asked as I stood and went to peek through a kitten-induced hole in my curtains. I should be on my guard in case other women showed up dead.

He didn't need to answer. Riley was on my front stoop.

I let him in because what else was I going to do? Riley had spent a lot of time here lately. Too much time.

"What came up?" I asked.

Riley ignored me, walking into the kitchen. He opened up the fridge door and grimaced.

"Why is it that every time I come over, you have the worst food ever in here?" He plucked a bottle of wine from the inside door and closed the fridge.

I put down the puzzle box and handed him two wine glasses. "You haven't answered my question."

Riley took a swig, emptying the wine glass in one swallow. Uh-oh. This was serious.

"The Agency wants me to check on the murder you stumbled upon last night."

"Does that mean you know who she is?" Maybe it wasn't so bad for him to be here.

He nodded. "It's the woman from the DC trip. Right?"

"That's right. Evelyn Trout."

For a second there, I was going to blurt out what Maria had told me about her really being a CIA agent. But I didn't want to get her in trouble. I'd wait and see what Riley had. I didn't have any qualms about getting *him* into trouble.

"Where's the body?" he asked.

"Is that why you're here? To identify the body?" I asked. "You met the woman in DC. It's the same one who died yesterday."

Riley shook his head. "No. I'm not here to identify the body."

"Then why did you ask?"

"Because I'm here to steal it."

CHAPTER SEVEN

———

Philby came into the room, and seeing Riley, jumped up on the counter and began rubbing her body all over him.

"She's *pink*!" His mouth dropped open.

"Yes she is. And so is my hair. You didn't even notice." I scowled.

Riley didn't take his eyes off the cat, who was now head butting his arm to get his attention.

"I already knew about your hair."

I looked around. "Tell me you didn't wire up my house to spy on me."

He shook his head. "No. Kelly told me."

Kelly. She and Riley had hit it off when they first met a year ago. She was always ratting me out to him.

"And she left out the part about the pink cat?"

"She did." He touched Philby, then drew back his hand to inspect it. When he saw that the color wasn't coming off, he started scratching her ears.

I told him about waking up to find the girls in the middle of dying my hair. Riley laughed. He really laughed. The bastard.

"It's a good look for you," he said. "But not for Philby, I think."

Philby purred in response, dropping onto her back and offering her belly to be rubbed. It was also pink. I had to admit—the girls were pretty good at this. And bonus—there wasn't any dye on the church carpets.

"I think she'd agree with you," I replied. "Now say again what you said a minute ago. You know, the thing that I hope I misheard?"

Riley poured another glass of wine. "You didn't mishear me. The Company sent me to retrieve the body."

"Okay, so why are you in my house? I don't work for the CIA anymore."

"I need your help." Riley gave me his most charming smile.

"First things first—how are you going to get the corpse? You don't actually think you can just walk in there, flash your credentials, and make off with it, do you?"

"Not at all."

"Good, because it's undergoing an autopsy right now. You'll have to wait." I grimaced at the thought of taking charge of a body that was currently cut open. That would be messy. I didn't like messy.

"And secondly," I continued. "I don't work for the Agency anymore. You seem to have trouble believing me on that." In the past year, I'd helped Riley like a million times. I was done. No more.

"Well first of all—I'm not here to ask for the body. I'm here to steal it. And secondly, you should help me. It's in your own best interest."

I folded my arms across my chest to process these two statements. My brain was fried, so I addressed the first point.

"You can't steal the body." I stuck my chin out to show him I meant business. "The police will then investigate that. And since I'm involved, they'll come after me."

Riley nodded. "That's a risk I'm willing to take."

And that's when I punched Riley in the arm. It was an excellent right hook, if I do say so myself. And it was very satisfying.

Riley frowned and rubbed his arm, which was now turning red.

"*I* am not a risk you are willing to take. You don't have that choice. It's my life. All mine and nobody else's. You can't tell me what to do anymore. Ever. I'm a civilian, and I'm not going to help you."

Riley grabbed some ice from the fridge, wrapped it in a paper towel, and applied it to his arm. Philby scowled at me.

Apparently she didn't approve of me attacking her personal kitty scratching valet.

"I apologize," he said. "I shouldn't have said that. I really don't want to put you at risk. But I do have to say it is in your best interest to help me. Evelyn attached herself to you. She died in your proximity. The powers that be are scrutinizing you right now. Once I take the body back to Langley—that unwanted attention will end."

"Great. Fantastic." The old saw was that when you left the CIA, you didn't really leave the CIA. I guess that was true.

"Maybe with the Agency. But here, the police department will come here first. I'll be their main suspect. And I don't need that right now."

"Hold on a sec." Riley held up one finger, then walked out the front door.

He returned with a suitcase. I toyed with punching him in the nose again, this time with more force in order to break it.

"No! You are not staying here!" I roared. "In addition to me not working for the CIA anymore, my house is not CIA property. You can't just commandeer it any time you want to!"

Riley gave me a look that implied that I was an imbecile. "I can't stay at a hotel. I need to come under the radar on this assignment."

"I'm serious, Riley! Rex lives just across the street! He'll know you're here. And when the body—the one that you are stealing all by yourself—goes missing, he'll know it was you."

He rubbed his chin thoughtfully. "We could always brainwash him."

I threw my hands in the air. "What 'we'? There is no 'we'!" I felt a vein throbbing in my neck.

"We're a team. We do this together or…" Riley stopped talking and rolled his suitcase down the hall to my guest room.

I followed. "Or what? What on earth do you think you have that will make me want to help you? I can't think of anything. Nothing."

Riley began to unpack. "Or I won't tell you who she is."

I started to say something, but closed my mouth. I opened it again. And closed it once more. I did want to know who Evelyn Trout really was. I wanted it so badly I could vomit. But did I want it bad enough to ruin my relationship with Rex?

"You're bluffing," I said. "You don't know who she is either."

He rolled his eyes again. "Then why am I here?"

I thought about this for a second. There was no way I could tell him what Maria had told me—that Evelyn had been a spy for the Company. And acting like I didn't care was right out. Riley would never believe that.

"I know who she is…or should I say, was?" Riley started to get undressed.

"Stop that!" I shouted. "You can't stay here, and taking off your clothes won't change that!"

The shirt came off. He looked good. Really good. Riley had an athletic body that, combined with his wavy blond hair and dazzling smile, was a deadly combination. In fact, it had worked on me a few years ago, when we actually were a team.

"I'm going to change. You can stand there and watch me, or you can wait in the kitchen."

My jaw dropped. I was about to tell him he wasn't intimidating me, until he took his pants off. I slammed the door behind me as I walked down the hallway, swearing. I couldn't remember being this angry, ever.

Philby walked to the center of the hall ahead of me and sat down, blocking my retreat. What the hell was this? Now my cat is giving me attitude?

I looked her in the eye and shouted, "Bob!"

Philby hissed loudly, falling over onto her back. She got back to her feet and with her chin in the air, trotted off, deeply offended. I felt bad. What was wrong with me? Riley pushed all my buttons, making me so mad that I verbally assaulted my cat.

I stomped off toward the kitchen, slammed my glass of wine and another glass before he came out and sat at the breakfast bar. Riley was partial to suits. He had them tailor-made in London. But now he was wearing a black polo shirt and khaki slacks. It was a good look on him. I looked down at my V-neck, T-shirt, and shorts and then poured another glass of wine.

"Tell me one thing that you know about Evelyn, and I'll consider your proposal," I said.

I wasn't really going to help him steal a body. But I needed to hear from him that the woman worked for Langley. Then I wouldn't worry about inadvertently giving Maria up.

"I'll tell you when you agree to help me."

I shook my head. "Not gonna happen. You give me good enough intel and I'll think about it. That's all I'm going to promise. And it has to be really premium information, too."

Riley looked at me then grabbed the phone book. I watched him as he pulled out his cell and ordered Chinese food to be delivered. He even remembered that I loved crab rangoons and sweet and sour chicken. The bastard.

"You're paying for that," I said.

He nodded, agreeing with me for the first time today…wait…tonight. It was night already. How had that happened?

The kittens came running in, and Riley scooped up Martini. She purred as he stroked her.

"They're big," he said.

"Quit avoiding the subject," I said, taking my kitten from him. If he wasn't going to be up front with me, he didn't get a kitten.

Riley had ordered from Ming's—the best Chinese place in town, and the fastest. Our dinner would be here soon. After he paid for it, I'd make him leave. I've kicked Riley's butt before. And I'd be more than happy to do it again. All he had to do was tell me Evelyn was a spy, and then I'd kick him out.

"You're withholding kittens from me now?" The man was actually amused.

I nodded. "That's right. No kittens for you. This isn't a petting zoo or a CIA safe house. This is *my* house. I make the rules."

Okay, so I felt a little stupid saying that while playing keep away with a kitten who looked like Elvis. Especially when I was begging for information I already knew. The only thing I didn't know was why the CIA sent Riley here.

"Why did they send you?" I asked, setting Martini on the floor. "Seems to me that if they really wanted this to be secret they would've sent someone no one here had ever seen before."

Riley shrugged. "They knew I'd just been here for the baptism. They thought I could find a way to stick around without it being suspicious."

"Well, Rex will think it's suspicious. He knows you left for the airport after the ceremony."

He feigned innocence. "What? You think he won't believe that I wanted to spend a little more time with my goddaughter?"

I shook my head. "No one is going to believe that."

The doorbell rang, and Riley walked out of the kitchen. He returned minutes later with two bags. The aroma was ridiculous, and I started salivating. In spite of my righteous fury, I pulled two plates out of the cupboard, and we opened the cartons. Riley handed me a set of chop sticks, and we started eating.

Oh wow. I've had Ming's many times, but it was always so good. Especially the sweet and sour sauce. That was my favorite. In fact, the crab rangoons and chicken were only there to sop up the yummy sauce.

Philby jumped up onto the counter and sat, waiting. I knew what this was about. This cat had a thing for meat. Any kind of meat. And she relied on the gross out factor to get it. She really was conniving. Once, she walked slowly across a plate full of bacon, then sat staring at me, willing me to stop eating. I didn't. Because…bacon.

But Riley might be different. He was a health nut. Having a cat interrupt his dinner by touching it might actually work on him. I wasn't going to stop Philby. Riley deserved it. I waited for the cat to make her move. Riley had a huge plate of Mongolian beef.

The cat did nothing. Nothing. She didn't even approach Riley. She just sat there, watching us eat. What was going on?

"Here, Philby." Riley tore off a piece of meat and handed it to the pink cat.

So that was her end game. Very clever of her to use the subtle approach on Riley. Or she had finally given up on me since I never gave her food.

We finished eating after Riley dispensed a few more "treats." I put the dishes in the sink and turned back to him.

"Your time is up." I pointed at him.

Riley wiped his mouth with a napkin veeeeerrrrry sloooowwwllly.

"Alright. I'll tell you what I know."

I folded my arms and waited for him to tell me something I already knew. I'd have to act surprised. I could do that convincingly for civilians. But would Riley buy it?

"Evelyn Trout was actually Vanessa Vanderhook."

My eyebrows shot up. I didn't know this part. But I didn't speak. I was saving the act for the big news. I was impressed that Riley had a higher security clearance than Maria.

"So? Who is Vanessa Vanderhook?" I prodded. Come on. Any time now.

Riley sighed. "She was with the CIA."

There it was. I gasped appropriately. This was all I needed to know.

Wait…he said "was." Was?

"Did you say she *was* with the CIA?"

Maybe he just meant "was" because she was dead now. It didn't seem that way though.

Riley nodded. "She was one of our best assassins."

My jaw dropped. That frumpy, dowdy, middle-aged woman was an assassin?

"Until she went rogue and dropped off the grid. The Company disavowed her. No one has seen or heard from her until she dropped dead at your sleepover."

"Movie night lock-in," I said absently. "But that's not entirely true. I'd seen her—in fact I'd shared a hotel room with her."

I brought my hand up to my mouth in horror. "I had a rogue assassin staying with my troop! You can never, never, never tell Kelly about this." And then I covered my mouth again. I'd just given him the ammo he needed to get me to help him. Dammit.

"I won't…if you help me." Riley grinned like a shark, circling.

"You met her in DC!" I tried to redirect. "Why didn't you say something?"

He shook his head. "I'd never heard of the woman until this week."

Did I believe him? I narrowed my eyes. I wasn't sure. He seemed to be telling the truth.

"I'm still not helping you," I said.

"We'll see," Riley said as he pulled out his cell and started pressing things on the screen.

"You wouldn't!" I reached for the phone, but he held me off.

Riley hit the speaker, and I heard the phone ringing. The top of the screen said "Kel."

Kel? What, he had a pet name for her? Oh, Kelly and I were going to have to talk about this.

I swung wide and Riley automatically brought his arm up defensively. He thought I was going for his nose again. But I wasn't. Instead, I hit his forearm hard, hitting the sweet spot that made him drop his phone. It fell to the floor, and I snagged it before he did, ending the call.

"I told you I'd think about it, and I have," I said. "I'm not going to help you. And not only that, I'm not going to lie to Rex if he asks."

Riley just stood there, grinning.

"What?" I challenged. "I said I'm not going to help you. Use your charms elsewhere."

"It's nothing." He waved me off.

"That's right," I said. "You have nothing. Nothing you can use against me."

"That's not entirely true." He cocked his head to the side. "I haven't told you everything."

"Whatever…you should go pack up now. I highly recommend the Radisson. You've stayed there before." I sounded confident. But something bothered me. Stupid curiosity. It gets me every time.

"Fine," I finally said. I have the patience of a gnat. "What is it you haven't told me that will make me go along with your stupid plan?"

Riley looked right into my eyes. "Vanessa Vanderhook left something behind."

"And?" I was tired. I needed this over so I could climb into bed with my pink cat and her kittens.

"A letter she faxed to the Agency the day she was murdered."

I threw up my hands. "So the woman can write? What of it?"

"The letter said that if something happened to her, Merry Wrath, aka Finn Czrygy, would be the one who murdered her." Riley leaned back against the wall with his arms over his chest.

CHAPTER EIGHT

"She may have said that, but it's not proof I killed her."

But if Evelyn were alive and standing here right now, I definitely would murder her. Most likely a manner with a lot of pain. Pain and pliers.

Riley sighed. "It's enough to make you the number one suspect."

I was so sick of this. My life since I'd left the CIA was nothing but one stupid murder after another, and I'd been framed more than once. Who'd think living in the middle of Iowa could be so dangerous?

"I don't even have a great alibi," I admitted. "Kelly was with me most of the time, but I'd waited for the pizza guy on my own for at least twenty minutes."

"So, establish an alibi for tonight, then sneak off and help me grab the body," Riley said.

"What kind of alibi could I have? You will claim you were never here, and I don't think they'll take Philby's word for it."

I really needed to start having someone with me at all times. Maybe I could hire an assistant who did nothing but give me an alibi. She could just follow me around twenty-four seven and say I was with her at that time. The idea did have some merit. I'd have to look into that.

But at this point, my head was spinning. It was too late to discuss this any further.

"If I help you, we're not doing it tonight," I finally said. "I need to sleep on it. You should too."

Maybe in the morning, Riley would see that this was a very stupid plan.

"I can't overstate the importance of doing this tonight," Riley said.

I silenced him. "No. I'm going to bed. There will be no discussion until tomorrow. The only one who'll listen to you tonight is Philby—and I doubt that she can help carry a body."

Pushing past him, I headed to my bedroom. Three sleepy kittens and their neon pink momma were curled up in the middle of the bed. After brushing my teeth and washing my face, I joined them.

And just in case Riley had some new pill to turn me into a zombie slave that would do whatever he wanted (you couldn't put anything past the CIA), I locked my bedroom door.

I awoke to the smell of bacon and eggs, and to the sound of my meat-obsessed cat pawing frantically at the door. I let her out, deciding not to warn Riley of Philby's little walking on bacon act. After a quick shower, I got dressed and made my way to the kitchen.

Riley was frowning at a plate of bacon. Philby sat a few inches away, tapping her tail on the counter.

"Your cat just walked across the bacon!" Riley seemed shocked.

Good girl! I picked up a piece and ate it. He looked a little green around the gills.

"She does that. Make sure you don't hold a burger too close to her either."

"Wow. Philby's pretty diabolical." Riley shoved the plate toward me and took out a fresh one, presumably for the rest of the bacon.

"When it comes to bacon, the Taliban has nothing on my cat." I sat at the breakfast bar and dug in.

Riley had made scrambled eggs, hash browns, and bacon. Or as I called it—the perfect meal. It was nice of him. But it was a trick. And an old one. Buttering me up with breakfast was not going to shake my resolve. I wasn't some stupid mark. I was a trained operative.

"So," he said as he turned the bacon on the griddle. "Have you decided that you're going to help me yet?"

"You're awfully confident." It was irritating that he thought I'd be so easy to manipulate. "No, I'm not going to help you steal Evelyn. That's a road I don't want to go down. I'm too established here. And because I want to continue living here without being constantly tailed by the police, I've decided that your plan won't work."

"Wrath, I…" He started to protest as he put out a plate with the last of the bacon.

I held up my hand to stop him. "I'm not changing my mind. I'll come up with some way to deal with this, and you can help me if you want to, but it has to be legit."

Philby was on her feet and trotting over to the bacon. I lifted the plate into the air before she could stomp across it. She was not amused. With an angry glare, she jumped off the counter and sat at my feet. She was counting on me dropping food, and she was out of luck. I never, ever dropped bacon.

"Do you have a plan?"

"No. But I think we have to tell Rex everything," I said.

"You're joking." Riley studied my expression. "That defeats the whole purpose of sneaking away with the body!"

I shook my head. "For the last year and a half, every time something like this has come up, I've lied to Rex. And he's tolerated it…but barely. I don't want to run the risk of him dumping me."

Riley didn't say anything. He collected up the dirty dishes and started washing them. I had no idea what he was thinking. My former handler and I had dated once. And I suspected there were still some feelings in there somewhere for me. But enough was enough. I wasn't going to lose Rex because of Riley.

"Okay," he said as he put the last dish in the drying rack. "Let's go see Rex."

I shoved Riley out the door as fast as I could so he wouldn't have time to change his mind. Even if he did, I wouldn't. I was going to tell Rex everything, no matter what. And the CIA couldn't do anything about it.

Okay, so they could do something. Like kill me or worse. But I didn't think it likely. At least, I hoped it wasn't likely.

We pulled in at the station and Rex was waiting for us. I'd texted him to make sure he'd be there. Apparently that merited curbside service. He greeted me with a grin and I called him *Detective* like he'd asked me to when at work. It was kind of cute and a little sexy—like a role-playing game—the detective and the Girl Scout leader. Maybe *spy* would be better. If he was surprised about my former boss's presence, he didn't show it. He shook Riley's hand and led us into his office.

I closed the door behind us before sitting down.

"What's going on?" Rex asked.

"The CIA wants to steal Evelyn's body," I said as I folded my arms over my chest and glared at Riley.

I didn't wait for Riley to change his mind or edit the facts. I told Rex everything. About Evelyn being a rogue assassin. Everything I knew, at least. If Riley knew more, he wasn't saying.

Rex looked from me, to Riley, and back again. I didn't think it would be hard for him to believe this. My boyfriend already knew about my past. And I didn't care what he did with this information, because I'd done my job. This was over as far as I was concerned.

Any minute now, he was going to let Riley have it just for thinking of stealing the body.

"So." Rex tapped a pencil on his desk and looked at me. "You let a trained assassin accompany your troop to our nation's capital?"

Okay, so I didn't think he'd see it like *that*.

"Well—" I hesitated. "When you say it like *that,* it does sound bad."

Riley had a flicker of amusement cross his features. He said nothing. Didn't even come to my defense. The bastard.

"And you." Rex turned on Riley. "You were going to steal the body and take it back to Spook Central?"

A little late…but there it was.

Riley nodded. He'd been a spy for so long he probably didn't see this as a bad thing. In fact, the CIA thought very little of the local authorities. To Riley, this was probably something Rex should give up as professional courtesy.

Rex buried his face in his hands. I knew this wasn't going to be the greatest moment. I just thought he'd be a little proud of me for being so responsible. I made a mental note to tell Kelly how responsible I was being, without letting her know about Evelyn's true background.

Rex sighed. "Well, at least for the first time since I met you—you're being up front with me from the start."

Okay, that stung a little. But he was right. And I was hoping to change my ways.

"So, what do we do now?" Rex asked.

"You could hand Vanessa's remains to me," Riley answered.

"Vanessa? Oh. Right. You mean Evelyn." Rex ran his hands through his hair. "I can't do this unless you step in, officially taking over the case. Which you can do. But for some reason, I don't think you want to do that."

Riley shook his head. "No. This is off the books. The Agency won't acknowledge it."

"Why don't you involve us in the investigation?" I asked. "Keep it all quiet, and when the case is wrapped, send the corpse with Riley?"

Riley nodded. "I could live with that—as long as it doesn't get out into the media."

What were the odds of that happening? I wondered. By now, ten little girls and their mothers also knew about the dead woman. I didn't think this case was quiet to begin with. My troop would at least brag to other kids about having a dead body at their lock-in. I had to admit that would be tough for any other eight-year-old kid to top.

"I can try…but only from here on out," Rex said. "We have a lot of witnesses, and half of them are underage." He looked at me. "I can't promise you that this isn't already out there."

Riley looked like he was going to object. But maybe he realized he was beaten. I had to give him credit—the man knew when to give in.

"Fine. We'll do it your way."

Yay! I shouldn't be happy, but getting these two to agree when I really had no master plan at all really was a coup.

Rex stood up. "You two might as well come with me. I'm heading to the morgue. The coroner has completed her autopsy." It might be the fastest that's ever been done in Who's There history.

We gave Rex a ride over to the hospital. The morgue was in the basement there, because they had the best facilities outside of Des Moines. Dr. Body was waiting for us when we arrived. I introduced them while trying not to trip her or throw her to the ground. This was proof of my amazing self-control.

"Nice to meet you, Riley," Soo Jin Body said, her mouth curved into a seductive smile.

Was this woman really trying to seduce him, or did she just always come off that way?

She led us into her office. I was a little disappointed that I couldn't see the corpse, but oh well.

"Drug induced heart attack," Dr. Body told us. "Acetylene. It was introduced by hypodermic. A huge dose— more than was necessary."

Great. It really was a murder. I'd hoped it would've been natural causes. No such luck. Someone had actually murdered Evelyn Trout, aka Vanessa Vanderhook. And that someone had tried to implicate me.

I was about to say something when I noticed that Riley and Dr. Body had sparks flying between them. I could actually see the sexual tension. And for some reason, it bothered me. Was I jealous? I should be happy that she's not flirting with Rex.

"Where was the injection site?" Rex asked, oblivious to the rarefied air around Riley and Soo Jin.

"On the back of her neck," the coroner said. "No defensive wounds or injuries. I'm pretty sure she never saw it coming."

"How soon before the drug took effect?" I asked.

"Almost immediately with that dose. Only a fraction of that would've been necessary to kill the woman." Her perfect, Cupid's bow lips curled into an impossibly seductive smile as she looked from Rex to Riley. Oh, how I hated her.

I pulled my thoughts back to the investigation. "No DNA? No strange hairs or fingerprints?" Could you even have fingerprints on a body? I wasn't sure.

Dr. Body shook her head. "Nothing like that. And even if we did have a strange hair, it would be nearly impossible to trace it. This isn't a TV show."

Rex and Riley laughed, and I felt like I'd just been set up. Was this woman after both men? I definitely had something to say about that. I knew how to kill her without leaving any evidence behind. And it wouldn't be acetylene either. Something bizarre, like a shark in her bathtub or a herd of runaway elephants.

"Thanks, Soo…" Rex glanced at me. "Dr. Body. We'll get in touch with you on what to do with the remains."

The coroner looked confused. "But the family has already claimed the body. I thought you knew that."

Wait…what?

Rex's jaw dropped open. "What are you talking about? I never cleared the release of the body."

Soo Jin looked on her desk and then handed him a sheet of paper.

"You authorized them to pick her up. They were here this morning."

Rex shook his head. "I never authorized this." That vein that throbbed in his neck—the one I thought was so sexy when we were snuggled on the sofa—was putting on a show now.

Dr. Body spoke up, "This is the right form, and there's your signature." She pointed a long, slender finger at the paper.

She knows his signature? She hadn't lived here or worked with him long enough to know that!

"It looks like my signature," Rex admitted. "But I never filled this out, let alone signed it and delivered it."

Dr. Body blushed and looked amazing doing it. I totally hated her.

"I'm so sorry. I thought this was legit!" Her eyes looked like they were going to well up at any moment.

Riley put his hand on her arm. I did not like that.

"Who's 'they'? You said 'they' came to pick her up. What did they look like?" he asked calmly.

Maybe he thought someone else from the CIA made off with Evelyn. I relaxed just a little. If this was the case, then it was all over. Riley could go back home, Rex could forget it all ever happened, and Dr. Body could meet with a terrible, disfiguring accident that would require her to move back to San Francisco. And then the department could hire a fat, ugly man to be the new medical examiner. Crisis averted.

"It was a man and woman. Both in their early twenties. Said they were the deceased's children. They had the correct paperwork," Soo Jin said.

She went on to describe two people who looked like millions of other people. Nothing had stood out to her. *She'd make a terrible detective*, I thought with an inappropriate amount of glee.

Most people would be flustered or at least feel bad about something like this. And I believed Dr. Body did. But she looked even more beautiful under these circumstances. Like a damsel in distress. I waited for these two men to light into her—like they have to me many, many times.

Riley soothed, "You did your job. No reason to be concerned."

Huh?

Rex agreed. "It's all right. I'll take it from here. Don't worry about it."

This time, my jaw dropped open. And remained open until we left the medical examiner's office. Then, I exploded.

"Are you two for real? She handed the body over to two strangers, and you guys are okay with that?"

Riley looked at me curiously. "It wasn't her fault, Wrath."

Rex nodded. "She did her job. And the paperwork looked legit. What do you want from the woman?"

Oh right. *I* was the jerk. How the hell did that happen?

"Dr. Body," Riley said, then blushed a little. Really? "Said they were average everything. Average height, brown hair, and so nondescript she didn't remember distinguishing features or eye color."

I snapped my fingers. "Dr. Body did it! She killed Evelyn! It's the perfect cover—moving to small town Iowa after San Francisco! Who does that?"

The men ignored me, and I was reduced to following them. Rex stepped up to the information desk and flashed his badge.

"Detective Rex Ferguson," he said with a grin to a tight-lipped woman. "I need to speak to your head of security. Can you page him for me?"

The woman nodded and picked up a phone.

"The hospital has security cameras," I said as I realized what was happening.

Rex nodded. "Yes they do. Even in the morgue."

A short, elderly man in a black security uniform rounded the corner and walked up to Rex.

"I'm Ted Dooley," the older man said. "You must be Rex?" He grinned in a very friendly way. I liked him. His hair and mustache were snowy white, and his blue eyes twinkled. They really twinkled. This guy could be a ringer for Santa.

"Yes." Rex seemed a little taken aback. "I'm Detective Ferguson."

The man looked flustered. "I'm so sorry. I shouldn't be so informal. I'd just heard all about you from my son."

"Your son?" Rex asked.

Mr. Dooley nodded. "Kevin. He's one of your officers."

Kevin the moron? Kevin had *parents*? Nice parents? I did *not* see that coming.

"Oh, yes." Rex smiled. "He's a good policeman."

Ted Dooley beamed and shook his head. "You didn't come here to talk about my boy, did you?"

"No, I didn't," Rex agreed. "We had an incident with the medical examiner. I'd like to see any security footage you might have from this morning."

Ted smiled. "Of course. This way." He turned and walked down a long hallway.

At the end of the hall was a glass door that said *Security*. We entered, and each of us stopped to stare. For a small hospital security department, they had a very up-to-date office. The latest computers and tablets filled every desk. A huge screen overhead monitored at least a dozen security cameras. The floor was carpeted, and the walls were painted a cheery yellow.

An aroma of fresh coffee filled the air, and a woman in a suit brought her boss a cup. She asked if we needed anything, but only Riley asked for coffee. Ted Dooley ushered us into his office. I thought Rex was going to have a heart attack.

Dooley's office was three times the size of Rex's. It had floor to ceiling windows and real paneled wood walls. The desk looked like something out of an office supply catalog for millionaires. The man motioned, and we took our seats in three extremely comfortable and newly upholstered chairs.

"Mavis?" Dooley punched a button on his desk. "Can you send me the footage from this morning?" He told her he wanted the tape from each and every camera.

The security chief barely sat back before Mavis appeared. It was the woman in the suit from earlier. She handed Dooley a flash drive and hit a button on the wall behind him.

A large screen unfolded from the ceiling behind us. We turned our chairs around to see a screen split into four, smaller screens. People came and went under the watchful eye of the cameras.

"Whatever you're looking for," Dooley said, "it'll be here."

We sat in silence as we watched. I was pretty sure Rex and Riley were flummoxed by the advanced technology here. I hadn't seen offices at Langley this richly appointed. We sat in silence, staring at the four parts of the big screen.

"No one can get in or out without being picked up by at least three or four cameras," Dooley proclaimed proudly behind us.

Apparently, it had been a slow day for the hospital, because there were very few people on the screen. That was good because it would be easier to identify our body-snatchers. A time stamp in the lower, right hand corner of each frame showed what time the footage was captured. We made it all the way through to the time it currently was, without seeing a couple—any man and woman together.

"Did you find what you're looking for?" Dooley asked behind us.

Rex swiveled in his chair. "Are you sure that's everything? We're looking for a man and woman in their twenties."

Ted Dooley frowned. "That's everything. I don't see how anyone could've come and gone without the camera noticing it."

"No one in this footage matches what we were told by Dr. Body," Rex said.

Riley and I didn't say anything. This was Rex's show, and we weren't going to intrude. But secretly, I felt the thrill of hope that maybe Dr. Body had lied to us. Maybe she took Evelyn! Then, she'd have to be arrested…oh no…

"Let's run it again," The security chief finally said.

So, we turned back to face the screen and watched again. But no matter how hard we looked, we never saw a couple who matched Soo Jin's description.

"Maybe they came separately?" Dooley asked.

I spoke up, "There isn't any footage of the body being wheeled out of here. Shouldn't that be on the tape?"

"Oh, wait a minute." Dooley punched a few keys on a keyboard on his desk.

This time, an image of one of the parking lots came up.

"You didn't tell me they were picking up a body. The morgue has a separate entrance for the funeral homes to drive up to."

Sure enough, a dark van came into view and backed up right under the camera. We couldn't see the rear doors, so we couldn't see if a body was loaded into it.

"No one got out of the cab," I said. "Do you think they did it all through the back of the van?"

After a few seconds, the van pulled away. There was no license plate, no markings at all on the van. It drove straight until it was out of sight.

"Whoever they were—" Dooley frowned. "—they were smart enough to avoid our cameras."

"Which means they'd done some reconnaissance to see where all the security cameras were," Rex said.

These two, whoever they were, were pros.

"This wasn't done by family members," Riley said.

I nodded. "This was done by professionals."

We thanked Ted Dooley and made our way outside to the car. None of us spoke—we were all trying to process what we'd seen…or hadn't seen. The drive back to the police station was almost equally quiet, except for Rex calling the station and putting an APB out on the van.

"Who do you think grabbed the body?" Riley finally broke the silence.

Rex rubbed his chin thoughtfully. "Do you think the Agency sent someone?"

"Not a chance." Riley scowled. "They sent me. And even then they demanded I keep a low profile. No, this isn't CIA."

"Feds?" I asked hopefully. But I knew the FBI wouldn't get involved.

"You said that Evelyn…or Vanessa that is, had gone rogue. Could it be another country that took her?"

Riley shrugged. "There's no way of knowing at this point."

"Ugh," I groaned. "More terrorists." That was all I needed.

CHAPTER NINE

————

We sat in the car, each thinking our own thoughts. It didn't help. On the one hand, this whole case was out of Rex's hands. On the other hand, someone bad was scooping up bodies in our little town. I didn't like bad guys here. This was my home.

Rex opened the car door, and we followed his lead, stepping out into the sunshine.

"I'm going in to call the airport," he said. "You two head over there and look for something suspicious."

I nodded. Riley and I got back into the car and hit the airport in ten minutes. I loved our little airport. It was small and homey but still had five airlines using it. Now it just seemed like terrorist central. Someone should have a discussion with them about the "no fly" list.

"You go to baggage handling, and see if anyone's checked a coffin," I said to Riley. "Your security clearance should get you through."

Riley agreed. "What are you going to do?"

"I'll walk around, see if anyone stands out," I said.

This was my training kicking in. I was pretty good at noticing things. If anyone looked out of place or spoke in a foreign language, I'd spot them. Besides, I spoke four languages myself, including Russian and Japanese. I entered the lobby and headed straight for the sitting area.

It was packed. That was weird considering it was almost noon. Most commuters flew early in the morning or late afternoon. I scanned the airline departures screen. There were three flights leaving in a few minutes. One was to Chicago, one to St. Louis, and one to Minneapolis. The Chicago flight must be it. O'Hare was the biggest international hub. You could fly out of there to Europe or Mexico.

I started walking around the seating area, trying to blend in. Unfortunately, all I had was my purse. I didn't look like a traveler. So, I acted like I was there to pick someone up. For ten minutes, I worked my way around the area, pausing to check my watch or purse, in order to eavesdrop. There were three couples flying who matched Dr. Body's description.

I sat down near the first couple. The woman was studying something on her phone, and the man was leaning back, eyes closed. He was far too relaxed to be the bad guy. These two didn't seem likely, and I was running out of time. Still, I took a discreet photo of them with my phone before moving on.

The next couple was a few rows over. I stood behind them, pretending to look for something in my purse, while taking more pics on my phone. In this case, the woman was constantly scanning the room, while the man was reading a novel. Half the couple seemed to be a likely candidate, but the other wasn't. In my experience, when the heat is on, people act nervous. This guy didn't have a care in the world.

The last couple was leaning up against a wall. They were locked in a very quiet conversation. I walked over and then bent down to tie my shoelace. I couldn't hear them well enough to decide what they were saying. Was this them?

I stood up and walked over to the opposite wall, leaning back against it, and while pretending to scrutinize my phone, took pictures of this last couple. It if was anyone, it was these two. Now, I just had to wait for Riley.

"Wrath," Riley said softly as he appeared next to me. "No one has checked a coffin or even anything as big as a coffin."

"Deal breaker?" I murmured.

"I think so. This is a dead end. Unless they stashed the body—which is highly unlikely since they went to such an effort to steal it—the people we're looking for aren't here." Riley put his hand on my back and we made our way to the parking lot.

"Rex?" I'd dialed him as soon as we got to the car. "Nothing here. Any news?"

"Nothing." Rex sounded frustrated.

I could understand that. "Do you want us to come to your office?"

"No. Head home. I'll stop over in an hour or so after I make some more calls." He hung up.

Riley and I stewed in our own thoughts as we drove back to my house. Who would have commandeered Evelyn's body? Was it someone she'd worked for? Someone who hated her? The possibilities were endless. Would we ever have an answer? I wasn't so sure.

Technically speaking, Rex could turn this over to the Iowa State Police. Or better yet, let the CIA handle it and send Riley packing. And while I liked that idea, I knew I'd want to know what had happened. It would be virtually impossible for me to wait on the sidelines for news that was too classified for me.

Whoever killed Evelyn also knew something about me. Enough to frame me in that fax to the Agency. That was disturbing. Even worse, they'd involved my troop by chucking her body at the church. Who were this mysterious man and woman? And how did they know me…or at least, something about me? A little thought crept out of the gloom inside my head.

"What if I was an assignment? What if Evelyn had been assigned to accompany me to DC?" I asked.

Riley thought about this. "It's possible. You could've been the target."

"And the body snatchers could be the ones who assigned her to shadow me."

"I like that idea even less," Riley said. "Because that means it's not over."

Great. He was never leaving now.

"Or…maybe she was hanging with me to hide out? What better cover than to hide with a bunch of kid tourists?"

Riley nodded. "I guess that's possible too."

Possible. I didn't like that word anymore. I wanted definitive answers on this. I wanted to know…everything! Why was that so hard? I considered these two options—one, that I'd been a target, and two, that Evelyn was hiding out.

"In both scenarios," Riley said, "someone is gunning for you."

He was right. I wished he wasn't. Why couldn't I just have a normal life with my lively Girl Scout troop and pink cat?

My cell rang.

"Rex?" I asked once I saw the caller ID.

"We found the van," he said. "It's parked at the high school."

"On our way!" I said before hanging up.

Riley and I made good time there. The van was the only vehicle in the lot. At least there wasn't any school today. We joined Rex at his car. Kevin was on alert, and by that I mean eating his way through a bag of cheese puffs while staring at his phone. How in hell could he be Ted Dooley's son?

"Did you check it out?" I asked.

Rex nodded. "No drivers and worse, no body."

I slumped. "Maybe it isn't the right car?"

"It's the right one," Rex said, holding out a baggie containing a rectangular piece of paper attached to string. "I found the toe tag."

I took the baggie from him. *Evelyn Trout* was printed on it.

"Fingerprints?" Riley asked when I handed the baggie to him.

Rex shook his head. "I don't know. I've got a team coming to process the van. We should know soon."

"Any witnesses?" I asked.

The high school was on the edge of town, surrounded by cornfields. Across the street was the 4-H complex where we held county fairs. On the next block was the school administration building.

"I don't know who we would ask," Rex said. "I sent Kevin to scout the fairgrounds for anyone, but he didn't find anything."

I glanced at Kevin, who was now smearing bright orange cheese dust across the front of his uniform. I doubt if Kevin could find his own head with both hands and a mirror.

"They must've met up with someone," I said as I walked around the van. "Whoever it was picked them and the body up here. Then they probably just took that road out of town."

Rex was talking to Kevin, who was listening while opening a bag of chips. He nodded and walked to his black and white. We watched as he drove off.

"There's a farm down the road," Rex said. "Belongs to Herbert Bailey."

I frowned. "How do I know that name?"

Rex shrugged. "It's an old farm. The same family has lived there for maybe one hundred years."

"Ah. Now I know who you're talking about. The Baileys had about a dozen kids. There was one in every grade."

In my grade was Seamus Bailey. He'd been an all-star everything. Nice guy.

"You think the Baileys might've seen something?" I asked.

"It never hurts to ask. It's still nice out. Farmers are always outside working this time of year," Rex said.

"Yes, but the Baileys are Irish Catholic. Working on a Sunday isn't something they would normally do," I replied.

Still, it was definitely worth a shot. At least it couldn't hurt.

Rex gave us the details of finding the van. Someone had called it in anonymously. I guess a strange, black conversion van in the middle of a high school parking lot on a weekend would seem pretty creepy.

Kevin's black-and-white pulled up, followed by a brand new blue pickup truck. The man who got out looked familiar. Probably my age, sun tanned with short, curly red hair. Yup. That's what the Baileys had looked like. All of them had red hair.

"Detective." The man shook Rex's hand. Kevin went back to eating. "My name is Seamus Bailey. The officer said you had some questions for me?"

Rex glared at Kevin. He was supposed to interview anyone he found at the farm, not bring them in. I wasn't surprised at all.

"Thanks for coming, Mr. Bailey. I really appreciate it," Rex said before introducing Riley and me as "consultants."

Seamus's eyes stayed on mine a second longer than necessary. He was probably trying to place me. It wasn't going to happen. My name had been Finn Czrygy when I'd lived here, and even if he saw through my new name and altered appearance, he wouldn't recognize me. And then I remembered that my bangs were pink. That must've been the reason for his strange stare.

I knew who Seamus was in high school, but I doubt he'd ever noticed me. One time, I dropped my math book in the hallway. He'd scooped it up and handed it to me without being asked. He told me I must be new and introduced himself. Even when I told him my name, he didn't recognize me—and we'd had classes together since kindergarten.

It wasn't his fault. I kind of encouraged this form of invisibility back then. And I wasn't keen on people finding out who I really was now. So why did it bother me? And what was with my over-sensitivity lately?

Rex told Seamus Bailey why we were there and asked if he'd seen any vehicles passing his farm.

"I was at church with my family until noon," He answered. "But I did see something at about one o'clock. It was a white truck hauling a horse trailer. No horses inside though. I remember that."

Of course not, because there was a body in the horse trailer. So that's how they did it.

"Did you recognize the truck?" Rex asked. "How about the people in it?"

Seamus shook his head. "It was a man and woman. But they were too far away to get a good look. As for the truck, there are a lot of white pickups around here."

Rex prodded for more information, but struck out. He handed the farmer his card and asked him to call if he remembered anything. Seamus nodded and left.

"Who transports a corpse in a horse trailer?" I asked.

Riley mused. "It's a good cover. They were smart enough to ditch the black van in an isolated spot."

A police van pulled up, and three people piled out. I recognized the faces of two of them, but not their names. I'm sure Rex introduced me, but I couldn't remember who they were.

I watched as Rex gave them instructions, and they swarmed the abandoned van.

"I'll let you know if they find anything," Rex said, before heading over to join the team.

"Might as well head back," Riley said.

I nodded. We wouldn't find anything more here. We got back into the car and found our way back to my house.

Riley and I spent the next two days glued to our cells and laptops. Rex didn't check in with us—probably because he had nothing new to say. Riley had called in favors from everyone he knew. I think he was upset to find out that here, in rural Iowa, we really don't fill the streets with security cameras.

Meanwhile, I researched Vanessa Vanderhook and came up with nothing. For the rest of the time, I pretended to search for clues, when in fact I was googling how to change your cat from pink back to white. I struck out there as well. I was doomed to have a pink cat forever.

CHAPTER TEN

———

Wednesday came, and I was relieved that I had a Scout meeting that afternoon. Kelly had everything organized, only needing me to come up with a few crafting supplies, which was weird, since at the lock-in it appeared she'd bought out the inventory of every craft supply store in a two-hundred-mile radius.

I ran a few errands and bought some stuff, arriving five minutes late. All of our meetings took place in the kindergarten room at the local elementary school, which was on the same block as my house.

"You're late!" the Kaitlins chorused as I walked through the door.

"Sorry about that," I mumbled before dumping the supplies on the table. Did you know that there are different kinds of poster board? Neither did I. Apparently there were nuances (and possible conspiracies) in crafting that I knew nothing about.

Kelly counted the twelve kids off into three groups of four. She told them they had to pick one girl in each group for this project. I sincerely hoped we weren't going to do trust falls again. That ended badly the last time when Betty's troop simply refused to catch her. I suspected that something was up, but the girls just pasted on their most angelic smiles and insisted they'd merely 'forgotten' what they were supposed to do. All four of them…at the same time. I'd had to break out the old first aid kid on that one.

"You will take these poster boards…" Kelly held up one of the oversized cardboard sheets. You have to be *really* literal with these girls. I didn't want them coloring on the walls, floors, or me. Once, they drew pictures of horses on the dry erase board…using Sharpies. It was our fault because we didn't specifically say, "Don't draw pictures on the stuff that isn't paper using permanent markers."

"And map out someone's life." Kelly waited for the girls to nod, demonstrating that they were, in fact, listening.

You really have to be careful because sometimes they nod, but they're really thinking about something else—like glitter gluing a window shut or wondering how many pieces of taffy will fit up Emily's nose.

"This is a planning exercise to make you think about the many places your life might take you someday, so that you can set goals and achieve them. As a group, pick one girl, and write a timeline, including any milestones she's planning for her future."

Emily raised her hand. "What's a milestone?" The others nodded.

Caterina rolled her eyes. "It's a stone that's a mile long…duh."

Betty shook her head. "It's a stone you can throw and hit something one mile away. Everyone knows that."

The other girls nodded solemnly at this sage wisdom.

Kelly decided not to respond to this, so I didn't either—mainly because I liked the idea of throwing a rock the length of a mile. You had to admit, that was a pretty inventive explanation. It was wrong, but inventive.

My co-leader walked to the chalkboard and drew a long line. She then drew shorter lines through it, writing a date at the top of each line.

"A milestone is a major event in your life. For example, near the beginning, you might have 'born' or 'started school.' These are things the girl has already done. In the middle, you will predict things this girl will do, like 'go to college' or 'get married.' And at the end, you'd have things like 'retire' or 'travel to Spain.' Things like that."

The girls all looked at each other for a moment before putting their heads together to choose who they were going to plan for and what those plans would be. I thought this was a great exercise. Kelly liked it because it was a teachable lesson. I liked it because I didn't have to come up with the idea.

"This seems to be going well." Kelly came over to me. "No one is fighting over who's in what group." She was right. The girls had calmly chosen someone without any bickering. That was a nice surprise.

"Where's the baby?" I asked. In fact, I couldn't remember a time since Kelly had given birth that I'd seen her without the infant.

"Robert's on daddy duty." Kelly smiled. "I needed a break, and he hasn't quite changed enough diapers yet."

"You call this a break?" I said, sweeping my arms around me. A troop meeting wasn't exactly my idea of relaxation.

Kelly shrugged. "I'll take what I can get. By the way— we need an idea for next time."

I thought this was the perfect opportunity to tell her about Lauren's mother's snail collection. Kelly looked horrified but didn't protest. She probably wanted a ready-made meeting too. And that's when I remembered the puzzle box. I pulled it out of my bag and showed it to her, explaining that somehow it ended up in Lauren's bag.

"That's strange." Kelly frowned as she took the box from me. "What is it? I don't remember seeing it at the lock-in."

"No idea. It's a box. And it has something inside. Something I can't seem to get out," I replied.

Kelly turned the box over in her hands a few times. Her fingers poked and prodded every spot, but nothing popped open.

"I guess we'll just have to ask the girls when they're done," she finally said, returning the box to me. "If we ask now, it'll just distract them."

I set it down on the table and waited. There wasn't any point in speculating what it could be if it belonged to one of the girls. Kelly and I sat in silence watching the girls color. Several of them stuck their tongues out as they worked. It's a good thing I never did that as a spy. Not only would I have looked like an idiot, but I would've had chapped lips.

I sat at a table while Kelly walked the room, answering questions. They didn't have many. Maybe they were old enough to understand directions now.

"Okay girls!" Kelly stood up and clapped loudly. Had it really been an hour already? "Time to choose a spokesman from your group who will tell us who you chose and what they plan to accomplish with their lives."

The four Kaitlins chose…you guessed it…one of the Kaitlins. One of the Hannahs was selected from another group, and the last one chose Betty. The Kaitlins went first.

"We picked Kaitlin." No surprise there, since the entire group was made up of Kaitlins. "This," Kaitlin said as she pointed to a timeline with very few lines, "is where Kaitlin was born. Then she went to school here." She pointed to another line, creatively marked *went to school,* and continued.

Kaitlin's timeline was fairly unimaginative, but it meant the girls understood the project. She was born, she went to school, got married, got a dog, bought a house, had kids, and died. Pretty common stuff. I was going to ask her about a job, but Kelly seemed pleased with the results, and the answer to my question could complicate things, so I said nothing.

Emily stood and revealed Hannah's timeline, with pretty much the same results. Nothing too interesting and definitely nothing about dying your leader's cat pink. This was promising. There had been no fistfights to break up, and no one cried or used four-letter words. It was almost boring. Sometimes boring meetings make the best meetings.

Betty's group was the last to go, and Betty rose, holding her board as Inez took her position as narrator.

"Here," she started, "is where Betty was born. Here is where Betty joined this Girl Scout troop. And here is where she met Mrs. Wrath's cat, Philby, and decided she likes cats."

Okay, that sounded more interesting. And I was kind of proud that one of the groups thought joining a troop was a big deal. It certainly had been a life-changing event for me. I was also flattered that Philby had made such an impression.

"Then, here is where Betty will graduate high school and go on to college to study cats," Inez continued.

I liked this board. These girls had put some thought into it. She pointed to a date exactly four years later and explained that at that point, Betty graduated and bought a cat. I felt a little proud that I was the one to introduce the girl to pets.

Inez went on. "Here is where Betty will be recruited by the CIA and sent to Afghanistan to make her first kill."

Wait…what?

"And here is when Betty has her first black bag drop…probably in Paraguay," Inez said as the girls in her group nodded.

Why Paraguay? I wondered. I had to admit I was pretty impressed with their knowledge of geography. But who was taking care of Betty's cat during her assignments? That was concerning.

"Um…" Kelly tried to interrupt, but Inez's momentum was unstoppable.

"And then," the girl said, "Betty will be elected President of the United States and invade Canada."

Well, that was interesting. I was just about to ask her what Canada did to incur President Betty's wrath, but the girl was on a roll.

"Here's when the zombie apocalypse will happen," Inez said as she pointed to a bloody stick figure.

Ah. That made sense to invade Canada. Because zombies freeze in the snow—everybody knows that. I looked at Kelly who seemed to be gagging. Apparently *she* didn't know that.

"After thirteen years as President, Betty will marry Mark Wahlberg and they will have two point five kids," Inez droned on.

Kelly regained the ability of speech in time to ask, "Two point five?"

I was actually wondering how Betty was able to get around the two-term law to have a thirteen-year presidency. And Mark Wahlberg would be a senior citizen by then, but maybe that didn't matter.

This time, Betty spoke up. "I saw that on TV once. The average American family has two point five kids. And because I'll be an average American, I'll have two point five kids."

It was pretty hard to fault her logic there. But I was pretty sure that the average American was not a CIA assassin who later became president and invaded Canada.

Lauren, from Hannah's group, asked, "How do you have point five of a kid?"

Inez fixed her with a sarcastic glare. "Well one gets half eaten by a zombie, duh!"

This was getting dark fast. I didn't say this to Kelly, but I kind of liked it.

Inez frowned and pointed at Betty's timeline. "And here's where Betty will die of old age at forty-two." She smiled and sat back down.

Ugh. This had shades of that Game of Life activity we did last year. Why was it so hard for these girls to confuse middle age with being a decrepit senior citizen?

"Forty-two isn't very old," Kelly said. "People live longer than that."

The four girls looked at each other before Betty responded, "Really? Cuz my mom is thirty-five, and she says she's dead on her feet all the time."

Kelly looked at me, and I shrugged. "How else could you interpret that?"

"Do we win?" Inez asked.

"This really isn't an exercise with winners or losers," Kelly said. I could tell she was gearing up for the wise leader discussion on why this was important.

"Why not?" one of the Kaitlins asked as the others nodded.

"That's not what this is about," Kelly insisted. "It's for thinking about life in general, and how you want to plan your future."

"I definitely plan to spend my future killing zombies," Inez said.

"Well," Kelly struggled. "Zombies don't really exist. And actually, most people won't go into the CIA after college…"

Betty looked disgusted. "I don't see why not!"

The room erupted into one huge argument as the three groups bickered over who had the best presentation. Personally, I'd have to go with Betty's group, but Kelly didn't ask, and I didn't think that now was the right time to volunteer my opinion.

Instead, I raised my hand in the air, making the silent sign. The girls all raised their arms to do the same thing, and sat down, waiting for one of us to speak.

"I think," I ventured as Kelly narrowed her eyes at me—what did she think I was going to say? "That this project showed that all of us have different goals for our lives. And I think that's good. Not everyone will go to college. Not everyone will get married. Very few will join the CIA, and really, none of you are going to die before the age of seventy."

The girls considered this for a moment before nodding and looking at me. I felt kind of smart coming up with that. See? I could interpret stuff like a responsible adult. I hoped Kelly caught that.

"Ladies." Kelly changed the subject and said, "Lauren found this in her bag after the lock-in." She held up the puzzle box. "Does it belong to any of you or your mothers?"

The girls shook their heads. "What is it?" Emily asked.

"None of you have seen it before?" I asked. "Are you sure?"

Once again, they shook their heads.

"What's on it?" Caterina asked. It was the first time she'd spoken all afternoon, but she was like that. She was silent as a grave most of the time. Caterina always caught me by surprise.

"I don't know. Are you sure you guys have never seen this before?"

One of the Hannahs walked over and took it from me. She touched two of the carvings on one side, followed by one on the other and one on the top. The box slid open.

"How did you know to do that?" I asked. "Is it yours?" This had to be like the underwear mysteries—no one claimed them even though they had to belong to someone.

Hannah shook her head. "I don't know. I just guessed."

I folded my arms over my chest. "You just guessed. You just...perfectly...in the right order...guessed exactly what to do to open the box?"

"Yup," Hannah responded, as if I was an idiot to ask.

"What's inside?" Betty called out.

A small, black pouch was almost invisible against the black velvet inside the box. I lifted the tiny bag out and opened it—shaking it over my palm. A small, black square landed in the middle of my hand.

"It's an SD card," Kelly said, staring at it. "Like for a cell phone."

I tucked the card back into the bag and shoved it into my purse. There was no way it was going back into the puzzle box. I hadn't paid attention to what Hannah had done. I wasn't going to be able to get it open any time soon.

"Never mind. It's probably nothing," I said. "Who wants to go outside and play a game?"

The girls were on their feet and standing in line at the door in seconds. Kelly and I led them outside and started them off with a game of tag. Watching the girls play was usually one of my favorite parts of the meeting. I learned a lot from them…who was shy…who was bold…who was creative…but my mind was on that little SD card in my purse.

I had my bag with me outside. I wasn't going to lose it until I could see what was on the card. Most likely, it belonged to one of the mothers and just had pictures and contacts on it. But until I was sure, I wasn't letting it out of my sight.

The puzzle box was, well, a puzzle. Why would one of the moms put a SD card in there? Why not just put it in the zippered pouch of a purse? It didn't add up. Unless whoever it was was very eccentric. My money was on perky, alien kidnapee, Carol Ann.

Or maybe it had something to do with Evelyn? No, that couldn't be it. Evelyn hadn't been in the church. She dropped dead outside. And the girls would've told me if they'd seen her. It had to belong to one of the moms.

The parents came to pick up their kids. Kelly showed each one the puzzle box, but no one admitted to being the owner.

"Maybe it's something from the church?" I asked my co-leader after the girls were gone.

She shook her head. "Those are pagan symbols on that box. No way they'd be in my church."

"Pagan symbols?" I frowned as I studied the box. "It's just nature symbols and maybe a couple of runes. What's pagan about that?"

Kelly rolled her eyes. "You don't know much about church, do you?"

"I find it interesting that you have to ask."

Kelly sighed the sigh of a thousand martyrs. "If it had crosses on it, that would be one thing. But this...this is totally different. Lutherans don't have much use for primitive symbols like these."

"What's so pagan about that?" I pointed to what looked like a bird.

"Trust me on this," Kelly said as she turned out the lights to the room. "I've got to get home and assess the damage."

"You don't think Robert can handle his own baby?" I asked.

Kelly grimaced. "I caught him throwing the diapers in the kitchen garbage instead of the Diaper Genie. And more than once he's mistaken the Cream of Wheat for the formula mix."

"What's a Diaper Genie?" I liked the sound of that. Was it a magic genie who made poopy diapers disappear? Did they do cat boxes too?

Kelly ignored me and walked to her car. She got in and closed the door. I could tell she was done for the day. My old friend didn't seem to have as much patience as she used to.

"Let me know what you find out on that card," she said, before starting the car and driving away.

"You aren't in the least bit curious?" I shouted after her, but she didn't respond.

Kelly's priorities had changed since becoming a mother. And I wasn't one of them. I'd have to figure out the deal on this puzzle box on my own. Sigh.

CHAPTER ELEVEN

———

I walked home and through the front door, only to find myself seduced by the smell of something wonderful in the kitchen.

"You're cooking?" I asked Riley as I tossed my bag on the counter.

He nodded. "I figured this was the only way we were going to eat something healthy."

At his feet, three kittens and one pink cat were staring up at the stove. I looked in the pot warily. How could it smell so good *and* be healthy at the same time? This had to be a trap.

"What is it?" I asked, afraid of what the answer would be.

"Relax, Wrath. It's just spaghetti."

"It'd better be as good as it smells," I warned.

He ignored me. So, I went and put my Scout stuff away while Riley continued boiling the spaghetti and baking the garlic bread. For a moment, I worried that the pasta was somehow made of vegetables and the bread was really tofu—but it smelled way too good to be what I called "fake food." There were two plates at the breakfast bar when I returned.

"How was the meeting?" Riley asked. It wasn't sarcastic. To my surprise, I realized he actually liked my girls.

This baby-loving, kid-liking Riley was something I was having trouble getting used to. The man used to avoid anything under the age of nineteen with a passion usually reserved for…well, me and vegetables.

"It was interesting as usual." I closed the puzzle box before taking it out of my purse and handing it to him. "Ever seen one of these?"

Riley took it from me. "I saw something like this in Norway once. I was seeing this stewardess named Hilda and she could do this thing with her tongue and right elbow that was…"

I held up my hand to silence him. "Yeah. I don't want to hear about that. Back to the box, please."

He pressed a few of the symbols and the box popped open. "Once, Hilda and her roommate, who was also named Hilda, had me over for a three-way. They liked to use mayonnaise…"

I snatched the box from his hands. "Like I said, I don't want to know."

Okay, so maybe I was a little pissed that everyone could open this stupid box but me. Or maybe I was a little jealous and didn't want the details of his Hilda squared sandwich. But it's my house, and I don't have to explain anything to him.

I reached into my purse and pulled out the bag with the SD card in it and handed it over. "This was inside."

Riley squinted at the small, plastic square. "Where's your laptop?"

I fetched the computer and watched as he popped it into one of the slots. Pictures flooded the screen. There were people I didn't recognize—kids making faces, a few selfies of some middle-aged woman, a couple looking over a table in a barn (antiquing probably—I hated antiquing)—stuff like that. Nothing unusual. But then, what had I expected?

I guess I expected suspicious activity. That's what a spy usually thinks when presented with such information. One time, in Tashkent, I retrieved a piece of microfiche (which was weird because who the hell used microfiche in this day and age?)—and instead of Russian plans for the latest stealth submarine, it had llama porn. That's right. Llama porn. I couldn't eat for a week without gagging involuntarily. Do not google it. Ever.

"It's nothing." Riley went back to the stove. "You should drop it off at the church."

"You think it belongs to someone there?"

Riley shrugged. "That's where it popped up, right?"

"Kelly says these are pagan symbols and it wouldn't be from the church."

"It doesn't have to be from the church to belong to one of the parishioners." Riley turned off the burners and drained the spaghetti. "You wouldn't believe the kinky stuff people take pictures of."

Images of the llama orgy popped into my head, and I shut it out while swallowing my bile. I'm serious. Do *not* google it.

"Why would someone store their SD card in a puzzle box?"

"Who knows why people do weird stuff?" Riley pointed toward the living room. "Why would someone use Dora the Explorer bedsheets as curtains for a whole year?"

Well that was a low blow. I'd liked those sheets as curtains. I always thought of Dora as an intrepid spy and Boots the monkey as her handler.

"Time to eat," Riley said.

Philby jumped up onto the breakfast bar, sniffing the air gently for meatballs. I lifted her back down to the floor, and she sat there, glaring at me. It's very strange to have a pink cat angry with you. Pink is such a happy color.

I prodded the puzzle box in between bites. There wasn't any *made in* label. In fact, there was nothing at all to indicate that this wasn't hand made. Maybe Riley was right—someone made this ugly little box just to store their SD cards. If so, they were probably looking for it.

Lauren didn't know how the box got into her bag, but that didn't mean anything. You could actually hand these girls something, remark on it, have them nod to acknowledge that you gave it to them, and they'd still insist they'd never seen it before. I call this "troop amnesia." And it happens whether it's a cookie order form or a permission slip.

I set the box back on the table. I'd give it to Kelly tomorrow and she could return it to whatever weirdo hid boring images inside a Scandinavian puzzle box. To be honest, I didn't care if I never saw the inside of that church…or any church…ever again. I would always associate them with pink dye and dead bodies.

"So what else happened at the meeting?" Riley asked.

"The usual. My girls never fail to surprise me." I told him all about it—especially Betty's future as a spy, and he laughed.

"I like Betty. Maybe we should start a program for kids—kind of like Junior G-Man."

I nodded. "My girls would make excellent spies. They're fearless and disturbingly creative. Maybe if agents are recruited and trained young, they'd be better at it than we were."

Riley frowned at me. "You weren't bad. I'm still good."

I rolled my eyes. "I was *great*. You're *somewhat* okay."

"Well," he said as he rolled an insane length of spaghetti around a fork, "I can certainly relate to the kids thinking people die at age forty-two. Some days it feels like I'm ninety."

I tossed a piece of garlic bread at him, and it bounced off his forehead. "You're only thirty-two. You're not that old."

"I don't know…I've been thinking of retiring in a few years." Riley looked off in the distance, eyes glazed over.

This was the first time I'd ever heard him express an interest in retiring. Riley was a lifer. One time he told me he was convinced he'd die in the field in his eighties. He probably thought he'd live that long because he ate so well.

"And do what, exactly?"

He shrugged. "Maybe private investigation. I could move here and set up shop."

My jaw dropped open and a little piece of spaghetti dangled from my lips. "Are you serious? You can't be serious!"

Riley as a private eye? In Who's There, Iowa? If we have this much trouble with one ex-spy working here, what would happen when we had two?

He looked a little wounded. "Why not? It seems like you alone bring in enough work to keep me busy for years."

I waved him off. "Not because I want to. Seriously—you wouldn't have enough to do here. And at the rate you go through women, you'd be bored in a month."

Riley ignored that. "What about Des Moines? It's only thirty minutes away."

"Why do you want to even be in the Midwest? If you were going to be a PI, you could go anywhere…New York City…Los Angeles…Dallas…anywhere."

The closest I was going to let him get would be Omaha. It was probably a hotbed of seething terrorist activity, right? In Iowa, we called it "Sin City."

"I like it here. I know people here. And I'm Finn's godfather."

"I don't think one of the requirements of being a godparent is to live here full-time." I was pretty sure I could find that in some churchy book, right? I couldn't ask Kelly though. She'd probably love to have him here. The traitor.

Riley grinned wickedly. "Maybe I'll do it just to keep an eye on you."

Something that felt like electric shock shot through me. It caught me by surprise. I might have mentioned earlier that Riley and I had once been a couple. When he came back into my life a year ago, there'd been some sparks. And recently, I'd discovered that our break up had been a complete misunderstanding on my part and that Riley still had feelings for me.

I didn't need that with Rex around. I didn't *want* that with Rex around. Did I? And yet, when Kelly told me that she'd asked Riley to be Finn's godfather, I'd felt a little flutter in my stomach. And just now, that little spark ran through me as I thought of him being here permanently.

"You're just saying that to get a rise out of me," I said at last. "You won't retire from the Agency until you're too old to dodge a bullet." I pictured a geriatric Riley (still with a full mane of golden hair, dammit) playing "bullets and bracelets" with an adamantium walker.

"I'm not so sure about that." Riley turned his full charm on me. The blue eyes and surfer good looks were hard to resist. Damn. Was he coming back here to be with me?

"Besides, I got some pretty serious vibes off Dr. Body the other day…" He grinned, and I considered stabbing him with my fork. This was exactly why I didn't want him here. Or in my life at all. I didn't like these mind games. Mind games should be reserved for Russians or Scandinavian, mayo-hoarding stewardesses—all improbably named Hilda.

On the other hand, maybe he could distract Miss Perfect Coroner and turn her attentions away from Rex.

"She's out of your league," I said, knowing full well that she wasn't. They'd be a gorgeous couple, and looking at them together would be like staring into the sun while mainlining Xanax.

Riley chuckled as he dumped another helping of spaghetti and meatballs on my plate. I didn't refuse it.

"And you'd have to find your own place to live because you can't live here." I tore off another piece of garlic bread.

"The house next door is for sale." He winked at me.

Oh crap. The house next door *was* for sale. It had been for a long time. That meant the owners would be eager to sell and take whatever Riley offered. With Rex across the street, it would be a bizarre love triangle. Literally.

He took his napkin from his lap and tossed it on the table. "But then again, I don't know if small-town life appeals to me. I mean, you don't have a decent restaurant, and there aren't any exotic places to eat outside of that one Thai place."

That's right…just keep thinking that. "And it's dull here. You'd be bored stupid."

Riley looked me right in the eyes. "I think you're wrong there. It's been nothing but exciting here for a while."

"I'm hoping that all this international intrigue will go away at some point soon," I said, even though I didn't believe it. Oh sure, I wanted it, but didn't believe it. Riley living here would just make matters worse. I didn't know how…but I knew it would.

"Well, I'm in no hurry." Riley started gathering up the plates. "As I said, in a few years…maybe."

I followed him to the sink with the glasses. That's when I looked down at Philby and the three kittens. Each one of them had little red goatees. My cats resembled little, furry vampires.

"You gave them meatballs?" I asked in horror.

Philby gave me a look, and then started grooming herself to get rid of the evidence. Great. Now in the future, he'd still give them food, but they knew to hide it.

"Better than having Philby sit in the spaghetti bowl," Riley said as he bent over to pet the cats. They purred and rubbed against his shins, plying their affection for marinara like pasta junkie prostitutes.

We washed and dried the dishes without saying anything. I was deep inside my own thoughts. I wasn't worried about Riley moving here…not really. Was I? My mind turned back to Evelyn. Was Riley right in thinking there'd always be lots of trouble in my vicinity?

I hadn't really considered it before, but trouble had found its way to me more than I'd ever imagined it would. When I was forcibly retired, I figured that coming back to this small town would be the answer to my problems. Things here would be quiet and as uneventful as a red-eye layover in Greenland. But I'd seriously misjudged. Somehow, international terrorists were dropping dead here like crazy.

What were the odds that Who's There, Iowa would become a hotbed of espionage activity, second only to Moscow during the Cold War?

We finished putting the last dish away, and together walked into the living room. I dropped onto the couch and rubbed my eyes. Riley sat down like a gentleman (the bastard) and was soon rewarded with a lapful of slutty, narcoleptic cats.

"So…" I said, a little uncomfortable with the silence. "Now that someone has taken Evelyn away, you'll be leaving now, right?"

He frowned. "Why do you say that?"

"Seriously? The reason you came here is long gone. There's no reason for you to stay."

Riley shook his head as he scratched behind Philby's ears. Martini, Moneypenny, and Bond were sound asleep, and their mother was cleaning up the last of the marinara sauce on their tiny chins.

"Until I know why she was here in the first place, and then who took her and why, I'm staying."

"Great," I said a little grouchily.

I reached for the remote and turned on the TV. I didn't watch it much, but it was the perfect distraction for moments like these. Oooh! Maybe the Royal Navy's field gun competition would be on! I stumbled on that in the middle of the night once. Men compete at carrying a huge, eighteenth century field gun over a series of obstacles. It was pretty awesome. What were the odds it would be on right now?

No such luck. The local news had just started. Oh well, that would do, I guessed. I stared at the two anchors. One of them looked familiar—the woman, not the man. She had glossy brown hair that hung in waves over her shoulders. We must've been in school together or something.

First Kevin, then Seamus, now this chick. My world was getting smaller as I recognized people from my past. Something spinning in my brain said we'd known each other as kids. It wasn't until her name was mentioned that I realized where.

"Lucinda Schwartz," I said, snapping my fingers.

Riley gave me a curious look. The cats were now draped, completely covering his body. I snagged Martini and she didn't even wake up. In fact, she was so limp I was afraid she was dead. How did cats do that? Why did cats do that? It didn't seem like a very good defense mechanism, since every feline I'd ever known (which was really just these four) had serious trust issues.

"We were partners in chemistry in the tenth grade," I explained. "See all that gorgeous hair?"

Riley looked at the anchor. "Yeah?"

"Well, I kind of accidentally set it on fire once. They had to shave her head. She wore hats for a year."

Riley laughed. "How did that happen?"

I felt a little guilty. "I moved that little flame thingy too close. Lucinda wore tons of hairspray then." I studied the screen. "And still does, apparently. Anyway—her whole head went up like a flash paper bonfire. Fortunately, the teacher grabbed the extinguisher in time. She didn't have any scarring or burns on her skin. Just singed hair." And the classroom smelled like a dozen witches had been burned at the stake in a room with poor ventilation.

"You were a menace even back then," Riley whistled.

I'd forgotten all about that incident. Lucinda never talked to me again—which wasn't much different from any other time. Kelly thought it was funny because Lucinda had been one of those mean girls who'd tormented her since elementary school. For some reason, after I'd set her on fire, Lucinda didn't go after Kelly anymore. I guess she was too afraid I'd light her up again. That was an unexpected benefit.

"She doesn't look much worse for wear," I mumbled.

Martini had begun purring violently while asleep. It felt like I had a running blow dryer on my chest.

"Our top story tonight," Lucinda intoned. Oh yes. I remember that rich, honeyed voice. Well... I remember it *screaming*. "President Benson will be visiting Willow Grove on a campaign stop. The president will be touring the fertilizer plant there—the largest in the country..."

Riley frowned. "President Benson is coming here?"

I nodded. "It's an election year. I heard his goal is to hit all ninety-nine counties in Iowa."

Ninety-nine counties. I always thought that was strange. Why not just divide one of the big ones into two for an even hundred? I'm sure it drove those with OCD nuts.

Lucinda droned on, and I studied the guy next to her. He didn't look right. Something was off. His hips seemed too high and he towered over Lucinda. Oh wow. He's sitting on a booster seat! The man's torso couldn't possibly be that long. The dude was short and using a booster seat to compensate. What was that about? I thought about mentioning it to Riley, but he was pretty vain himself. He'd probably just sympathize with the guy.

"I don't know the other anchor," I mumbled. "He must not be from around here." I wondered if I ran into Lucinda, if she'd remember me. Probably not. That was a long time ago.

"Firefighters across the county came together today..." Short Anchor Guy said.

The image of a farm on fire came onto the screen. Lucinda winced a little. I guess she would remember me after all.

"...Mr. Seamus Bailey was found dead..."

Riley and I sat up straight, our eyes trained on the screen.

"...in what appears to be an act of arson. Local firefighters wouldn't comment with the investigation pending, but sources tell us the Bailey farm was deliberately set on fire."

Oh no...

The fire chief came on screen. "We found some suspicious activity. It wasn't consistent with what was going on at the farm at the time."

Riley and I glanced at each other for a split second before turning back to the TV.

"Mr. Bailey's body has been sent to the coroner's office for examination. Stay tuned for updates…" Lucinda's voice faded out as I realized what had just happened.

"Do you think…?" Riley asked, but I already had my cell out with my fingers finding the favorites in my contact list.

"Rex," I said when he answered. "We just saw it on the news." I hit the speaker so Riley would hear.

"I was just about to call you." My boyfriend sounded tired.

"How is Seamus's family?" Seamus had been a nice guy. This was so wrong.

"They're okay," Rex said. "They weren't there. His wife and kids were visiting her father in Winterset when it happened."

"That's good," I said.

"It's definitely deliberate, Merry." Rex sighed. "I'm going to stay here until the fire marshal is done. Then I'm heading to the morgue to see what Dr. Body found out."

"Okay. Let us know."

"It'll probably be tomorrow morning," Rex said. We exchanged goodbyes, and I hung up.

"Riley," I started to say, but my mouth felt like it was full of cotton.

"I think so too." His face was grim.

"Just because he saw the truck and horse trailer…" I said.

Riley said nothing. We just stared at each other. And that's when I'd decided that these killers had just signed their death warrant. Because now, I was bringing the wrath of, well…Wrath.

CHAPTER TWELVE

———

I didn't sleep well. A reel kept spooling over and over with Seamus talking to us, the fire at the farm, and the look on Riley's face when he realized it was due to Evelyn's disappearance. Oh, and occasionally I would see Lucinda's head on fire, but that wasn't every time. I'm not a *monster*.

What I was torturing myself with was the fact that Seamus's wife and kids were now without a husband and father. And no matter how I spun it, I couldn't help thinking it was my fault. Riley had poured us both a healthy belt of Scotch after the news hit. I didn't even know I'd had Scotch. And this was thirty-year-old Oban. Thank you, Scotch Fairy.

Were the killers going to come after me? I hoped so, because I looked forward to killing them…slowly…with a lighter and rusty nail clippers. There's a reason TSA won't let you take them on a plane—and it's not what you think. Normal people don't know how to kill someone with manicure implements, but *I* do.

With the way things were going, I worried that Kelly and her family or the girls in the troop may become targets. That made me toss and turn.

Since I clearly wasn't going to sleep at four a.m., I got up, showered, dressed, and fed the cats—who were clearly confused to be eating breakfast while it was still dark outside. They didn't argue, though.

I sat in the living room with a cup of tea and my laptop—scanning for updated news. There wasn't any. This wasn't the big city with twenty-four-hour news feeds. At five a.m., Riley joined me, also showered and fully dressed.

"Anything new?" Riley asked sitting down with a cup of coffee. I didn't even know I owned a coffee maker. Was he buying appliances for my house?

Four cats came flying to him as if he was magnetized. Was he giving them coffee too? I'd need to talk to him about that. The last thing I needed was nervous, wide-eyed felines vibrating in place.

"Nothing." I turned off the television and turned toward him. "Do you think they'll be back?"

I hoped so. While I was getting ready, I found a rusty nail file by the tub and added it to my torture tools. The killers were so doomed.

"The body snatchers? I don't know. I didn't think they'd come back." Riley put the kittens on the couch between us but kept Philby.

"So they saw Seamus as they were leaving town and decided to finish him off?"

Riley's mouth formed a tight line. "It looks like that."

I shook my head. "But that doesn't make any sense. They were gone. In the clear. No one knew who they were or where they were going. And they had to know the police would interview Seamus. Why kill him after he described them?"

"Criminals make mistakes," he said. "It happens all the time."

A realization came over me and made me grumpy. "I guess this puts the case back under Rex's jurisdiction." That meant Riley would stay.

"That's true," Riley agreed. "You know what this means, don't you?"

I tensed up, fearing the worst. "What?"

"We need to go shopping and get some groceries for the long haul."

"The long haul?" I asked. "Does it have to be a long haul? I mean, Rex is perfectly capable of handling this."

"You forget—" Riley gave me a look I couldn't read "—that the Agency sent me here to recover Evelyn's body. That's my mission. I'm supposed to return with it. So like it or not, Wrath," he said with a toothy grin. "I'm not going anywhere until this is over."

He winked at me. Fantastic.

We got two carts at the store because he was going to look for healthy food, and I was hitting all my staples, which included Pizza Rolls, three cheese ranch dressing, Oreos, and Hostess *everything*. We separated, primarily because the aisles we were looking for were separated by paper products and laundry detergent.

I was lifting a heavy box of cat food off the shelves when Kelly turned into my lane. Finn cooed adorably from her car seat in the front of the cart.

"I just saw Riley." Kelly threw her thumb over her right shoulder. Looking into her cart, I could see why. She had a nice, balanced set of fruits and vegetables. *Show off.*

"Yeah." I wiped my forehead. "I guess he's staying with me for a while."

Kelly looked at me for a moment. "What's going on?"

This was it. The moment of truth. I'd have to tell Kelly about Evelyn being a rogue assassin. She wasn't going to like it and it would undo all that work I've done to reestablish myself as a responsible adult in her eyes. How much could I tell her without telling her *everything*?

"Riley's here on an investigation that happens to be tied to that fire at the Bailey farm last night."

Kelly's face crumbled. "That was horrible. I saw that on the news. Poor Seamus."

"I saw it too. I couldn't believe it. He was such a nice guy back in high school."

"That's why I'm here," Kelly said. "I'm going to make a casserole for the family. I guess they're staying with Seamus's cousin."

Ah…Kelly's famous tuna noodle casserole. My mouth began to water. Maybe if I pouted, she'd make me one.

"How is that tied to a CIA investigation?" she asked quietly. Finn had fallen asleep.

It was the moment of truth. I'd have to tell her sooner or later.

I chose later. "No idea. He's working with Rex, and I'm sitting this one out. Hey! Did you see Lucinda flinch when she saw the fire?"

A slight grin crossed my best friend's features. "I did. I think she was wearing extensions. So dangerous. Very flammable."

I'm not embarrassed to say I laughed out loud.

"I've got to get back," Kelly said as she looked at her watch.

"How's maternity leave going?" I asked.

For a second, I thought I saw something in her eyes. Kelly was an emergency room nurse at the hospital. I wouldn't be surprised if she said she missed it.

"Great. I stopped by there this morning to show off the baby. I guess they've got a new coroner now."

I steeled myself. "Dr. Soo Jin Body. We've met."

Kelly looked at me with interest. "What's wrong with her?"

I shook my head. "Nothing's wrong with her. That's the problem."

Kelly narrowed her eyes. "Spill it. You can't hide things from me."

Well, so far I'd been keeping the news about Evelyn quiet…

"You got me." I let out a rush of air as if I'd been holding my breath. "She seems a bit familiar with Rex. And she was flirting with Riley too."

"Rex is into you, and no one else. And Ri…wait…"

Uh-oh.

"Why did Riley meet her?" This time she folded her arms.

My mind scrambled, trying to come up with a reason, but I had nothing. I was much quicker in my spy days. But Kelly would've made an excellent spy. And human lie detector. There wasn't any point in avoiding it any more.

"Hey Kelly!" Riley turned the corner and upon seeing Kelly, hugged her warmly. "And Finn! My two favorite ladies!"

Kelly smiled at him and nodded at the baby. Riley gently stroked the two-month-old's cheek without waking her up. He looked into her cart.

"Is that…?" His eyes locked onto the canned tuna. "Are you making your fabulous tuna noodle casserole?" Riley, who never ate anything from a can, was smitten with Kelly's casserole.

"Yes, but it's not for you. It's for the Bailey family," Kelly said, slapping his hand as he reached for the pasta.

Riley poured on his ten thousand watt smile—a smile that melted the panties off of many a super model.

"It's so good to see you both!" he said smoothly. "Hey Wrath, we've got to go. This stuff is fresh and it won't keep much longer." He pointed to his cart, which was filled with things I had no idea even existed.

"I'll call you!" I shouted over my shoulder as we made our getaway. Kelly didn't respond.

"How did you know she was about to pounce on me?" I mumbled to Riley in the checkout line.

He pretended to look wounded. "I *am* a spy."

"Well your timing was perfect," I said as we started unloading his cart onto the conveyor belt.

"You can't hide the truth from her forever," Riley said quietly as he looked around to make sure we weren't overheard.

I nodded. "I know that. But every moment that I can put it off makes life easier for me."

Once the groceries were bagged, we rolled them to the car and unloaded them into the trunk. I didn't relax until we were in the car and on our way back home.

"Just have her come over so you can tell her face to face. And maybe ask her to bring a casserole…" Riley said, keeping his eyes on the road.

"She probably realized two seconds after we'd left that she'd been played." I scrunched down into my seat, as if that would make me invisible. Wouldn't it be great if shrinking in your seat really did render you transparent?

Riley scratched his chin thoughtfully. "I don't know about that. Women who've just had babies tend to be distracted for months afterward. All of her attention is going to the kid now."

I stared at him. "How do you know that?" *I* didn't know that!

"It's evolution. A mother's body is hardwired to focus only on her child at this time. Her only role in life is to keep Finn alive and healthy."

"How do you know that?" I repeated.

He continued as if I hadn't spoken. "It's mother nature dictating her priorities. She can't help it."

I punched him in the arm. "Riley—how do you know this stuff?"

He gave me a curious look. "I've been reading up since Kelly asked me to be Finn's godfather."

"You? You've been reading up on babies. You."

To be perfectly honest, this announcement shocked me more than that time when I caught a Chechen terrorist practicing ballet positions when he was supposed to be guarding an armory. He'd even made himself a little camouflage tutu.

"Yes, Wrath," Riley said a bit defensively. "I studied up. That's what we do in our line of work. Get prepared for anything the job throws at us."

"You're weird," was my mature reply, and I turned my head to look out the window.

We didn't speak until all the groceries were brought in and sitting on the counter, under the supervisory eye of Philby. When she realized Riley hadn't bought any meat, she gave him a withering look.

"What is this?" I held up a container of tofu. I hated tofu.

"We were stationed in Japan, so I know you know what tofu is." Riley took it from my hands and put it away.

"I have no idea how to cook half of this stuff. Let me rephrase that—your half of this stuff."

"You won't have to," Riley said as he put bundles of fresh veggies in the crisper. "I'll do the cooking."

I threw my hands up. "I don't get what it is about my house that makes you think it's yours. Why aren't you staying in a hotel now that Rex knows why you're here?"

Riley flashed a quick smile. "And miss out on this scintillating conversation and—" he held up a can of SpaghettiOs "—the joy of your eclectic taste in food?"

I snatched the can from him. "I should charge you rent."

"Okay," Riley said as he put the last of his weird food away. "As it is almost lunchtime and in an attempt to pay you back, I'll take you to lunch. Your choice. Anywhere you want."

"It's a deal." And he was totally going to regret it.

CHAPTER THIRTEEN

———

I grabbed the keys and led him out to the car. There wasn't any point in telling him where we were going. He'd just find a way to fight me on it, and I've incapacitated him before—I could sure as hell do it again. I was just too lazy to carry his inert body to the driveway.

"Pizza?" Riley said as he saw the blinking sign.

"No," I said as I put the car into park. "Tony's Pizza—aka the greatest pizza in the universe. There's a difference."

We sat down and ordered lunch. Tony's was one of those tiny Italian restaurants with dark wood walls and red and white checked tablecloths. Tony's wife waited tables while his son delivered pizza.

"Merry!" Carla Vincente said as she set down two glasses of water in front of us. "The usual?"

Riley's right eyebrow went up, but he said nothing.

"Not today, Carla. We'll need a minute."

Carla gave Riley the once-over. She usually saw me here with Rex. She said nothing but moved on. Carla was great, but a bit judgey. I had no doubt Kelly would be hearing about this soon. I handed Riley his menu, and he opened it. The smells of what pasta heaven must be like wafted from the kitchen.

I already knew what I wanted, so I had a little time to think while Riley read through the options. I was a bit distracted over our current roommate situation and wasn't sure I wanted to discuss it. What was there to say? Nothing I'd said yet dislodged the man from my guest room. It was obvious I'd have to put up with us living together.

Wait…living together? Where had that come from?

"Ms. Wrath? Mr. Andrews?" Dr. Body was standing over us. She wasn't dressed in her work garb, instead looking ridiculously adorable in capris, a T-shirt, and sneakers. How I hated her.

"Dr. Body!" Riley stood and pulled out a chair for her *without asking me*. "How nice to see you. And please, call me Riley."

I wasn't surprised when the woman sat down. To be honest, I found myself a little dazzled in her presence. She was too flawless to be real. If only she had crooked teeth, or acne scars, or ugly clothes. Sadly, no matter what this woman did, she was still gorgeous.

"Sorry about my appearance. I took the day off to get some work done in my new house. And please...call me Soo."

Riley turned to glare at me. Oh, what the hell.

"It's Merry. Please call me Merry," I gave my best undercover smile usually reserved for whomever I was just about to kill.

"Thanks for letting me join you. Ted Dooley at the hospital recommended this place."

"We're about to order a large pizza—feel free to join us on that," Riley said smoothly.

Hey! This was my pizza! I didn't want to share it with a beautiful she-demon who was after my men!

"Great idea," I managed. Well, I am a good actress.

"Thank you!" Soo smiled, and I was pretty sure it turned the dark restaurant into day.

Carla appeared, pad and pen in hand, and I ordered the Milano. Double pepperoni and sausage, it was my favorite. Riley and Soo Jin didn't protest.

"So, how are you settling in?" I asked with a smile that didn't quite have the same wattage. It was more like a dim bulb.

"Easily. Everything is so much easier here than it was in San Francisco. Just finding affordable housing in the Bay Area can take months."

"Were you a medical examiner back there?" Riley asked. He may not have realized it, but he was definitely pumping her for intel. And that was the only thing I wanted him pumping.

Soo nodded. "I was. You know, I thought things would be much quieter here. But in the last twenty-four hours, I've had two bodies—both homicides."

"Seamus Bailey," I said softly. I felt a stab of remorse. Here I was cleverly imagining the doctor's hideous death, and Seamus was murdered for just being outside at the wrong time.

"Did you know him?" Soo asked.

"I went to school with him…back in the day." Geez, I sounded like one of those ancient farmers who hang out in the local diner at five in the morning.

"I'm so sorry." Soo turned her soothing, brown eyes on me, and to my surprise I felt my sadness slipping away. Maybe she was an evil hypnotist.

I waved her off. "It's okay. I haven't seen him since high school."

Riley decided to change the subject. "Sounds like you're settling in okay."

Soo seemed grateful for the diversion. "I am. Everyone has been so nice. Like you, Rex, Ted Dooley, everyone!"

Hmmm…did she even realize she was only naming men?

"I like it here. I don't think I'll ever go back to a big city environment."

I spoke up, perhaps a smidge too enthusiastically. "Oh? You don't think you'll get bored here?"

Riley glared at me. "I've been thinking of retiring here. Maybe starting up a business."

Soo looked from me to Riley. "You're pretty young to retire. You work for the CIA, right?"

Normally, Riley would've cringed hearing that out loud. We were trained to be discreet. Except I noticed that anything Soo Jin said was exempt from the norm.

"At some point—" he gave her a slow, boyish smile "—a man wants to settle down, start a family, that kind of thing. Who's There seems like the best place to do that."

What? Riley wasn't the starting-a-family type. At all. But apparently, something about the good doctor had him all melty.

"Don't mind him," I said smoothly. "He's just become the godfather of a baby here. It's his first experience with settling down."

Dr. Body laughed. It sounded like wind chimes ringing. I had to admit, her charms were starting to work on me too. We made small talk for twenty minutes, and I was starting to relax. This wasn't too bad. Notice that I didn't say Soo Jin wasn't too bad. But the conversation passed the time.

"Here you go." Carla set down a giant thin crust pizza cut up into three by three inch squared pieces. "Enjoy," she said as she walked away.

"Whoa!" Soo said, staring at the pizza in awe.

"I know, right?" I was giddy as I scooped up several squares on my plate. "This is the best pizza in Iowa."

Riley frowned. "What's that liquid on top?"

"Grease," I said through a mouthful of cheesy and meaty goodness.

Soo and Riley exchanged glances. Neither one made a move to take a piece. Maybe I'd get lucky and they'd order something else. And I'd have the pizza all to myself.

"Is it edible?" Soo asked, while Riley took a few pieces and began blotting them with a napkin.

I stared at them. "Of course it's edible. I grew up on this, and I'm fine." What was wrong with these two? "And don't blot the grease, Riley! It's necessary for the flavor."

His eyes grew wide. "It is? How is grease necessary for anything?"

To her credit, Soo Jin sucked it up and helped herself to several pieces.

"Well, I'll give anything a shot at least once." She popped a square into her mouth. She was still for a moment, then her eyes closed and she moaned.

"Wow. It is good. And you're right about the grease!" she gushed.

Okay. So I liked her a little now. I turned my attention to Riley. He looked at his plate and finally picked up a square and took a tiny nibble. I was on my eleventh piece already.

"I mean, this isn't what I'm used to," Soo said. "We're pretty health conscious in San Francisco. But this is wonderful!"

I nodded. "I've been to the City by the Bay. Wait till you hit an Italian place here. You can stand a fork up in the alfredo sauce."

I loved San Francisco. But I didn't love the food. Too healthy. The alfredo sauce there looked just like wet noodles. After a few days I found myself practically crawling into a dark hole-in-the-wall and begging for a greasy burger with heaps of melted cheese. When I asked them to put cheese on my fries, and then dipped them in ranch dressing, a woman fainted.

Good stuff.

Soo laughed. And it was the most charming laugh in the history of charming laughter. It was really hard not to like her. Jealousy seemed to be my primary motivation. But that wasn't very fair. And what's wrong with her flirting with Riley? I had Rex. And I was over Riley. Totally.

"This might be inappropriate, and if so, I'm sorry." Riley placed his hand over his heart and turned the charm up to eleven. "But Detective Ferguson filled us in on Seamus Bailey."

Dr. Body nodded and popped another piece of pizza into her mouth. Riley took that as approval.

"Did he die from smoke inhalation or the burns?" He pasted on his saddest look.

"Neither," Soo said as she wiped the grease from her fingers.

Riley looked confused, "Neither? Then what did he die from?"

Soo looked from Riley to me. "I just told Rex, so I guess it's okay to tell you. He died of a gunshot wound to the back of the head."

"He was shot? Then the fire was merely camouflage!" I said.

Soo nodded. "From the angle of penetration, I'd guess that he was shot execution style and at close range."

I slumped in my chair. Well, that sucked. That meant this mystery couple was way more dangerous than we'd thought.

"Thanks for telling us," Riley said, and Soo almost started purring. He had that way with women. He'd had that way with me once too.

There was an uncomfortable silence. The pizza was nearly gone. I guessed I wouldn't be taking any home.

"I have a professional question, Soo," I said. "Does working with cadavers dampen your appetite? Because it would mine."

Soo laughed. "Not really. I've got a pretty strong stomach. And I'm used to it."

Used to it? Who gets used to it?

She saw the confusion in our eyes and smiled. "My dad was an anatomy professor at a California medical school. I've been around dissected people since I was twelve."

Okay, that was weird. I was sorry I'd asked. Who drags their kid along to dissect humans? Her dad sounded a bit like a psycho.

Riley stared at her. "That's fascinating! So that's why you decided to become an M.E.?"

"Well, that and I'm basically pretty shy," she said.

Riiiiiiiiiiiight.

Soo continued, "So being around dead people all day is more relaxing than having to make conversation all day."

She seemed to have no trouble with that now.

"That's an interesting way to look at it." Riley grinned.

No it wasn't. It was just another way for Riley to try to seduce her. My former boss had a talent for putting people at ease and making them feel like the most fascinating person on earth. It was a gift for a CIA operative. And a necessity for a seducer.

"Are you all moved in?" I asked as I kicked Riley under the table.

Soo took a drink of iced tea before answering. "I think so. My house is on an isolated stretch of road on the edge of town. Very peaceful. But also lonely."

What? She just told us she was shy and didn't like being around people.

"Do you like cats?" Riley asked.

Uh-oh. I had a bad feeling where this was going.

Soo clapped her hands in delight. "I love cats! I wanted to get a pair of kittens in San Francisco, but I was too busy and worked a lot of hours. But now, things are much slower here. I should definitely look into it."

"Look no further." Riley smiled. "Merry's cat just had kittens. And they're weaned. I'd bet she'd love to give you two of them."

It was all I could do not to jump out of my seat and snap his neck. Really? He was giving my cats away? And to *her*?

"Ooooh!" Soo cried. "I'd love to see them! Would you really part with a couple? That would be perfect!"

"Well, actually, I…"

Riley cut me off, "Why don't you stop by now? We're just heading home anyway."

"Uh, Riley, don't you think…" I tried again.

"I would love that!" Soo squealed. "I'll just follow you home!"

I tried to think of something to say. I really did. But my mind had been blown and wouldn't be itself for a while yet. Why did Riley do that? They weren't his cats. And it wasn't his home! This was getting way out of hand. But what could I do? I had to follow through with it.

Riley paid the bill and as we walked to our car, said, "I'll ride with you, Soo. That way if Merry loses us, I can get you there."

"Thank you," Soo enthused. "I know it's not a city, but I still haven't fully found my way around yet."

So, there I was, driving my car back to my house with Soo and Riley trailing behind. I toyed with slamming on the brakes so they'd rear end me. Or maybe I could call Kelly and have her run over and hide the kittens. Anything to keep this woman away from my cats.

Oh, come on, Wrath, I thought. She's not a bad sort. She's smart and ugly-challenged. Soo would probably be a good owner. But still, they were my kittens. And how would Philby take losing two of three of her babies?

The thought made me sad. For a moment I thought maybe I could lose her car. But Riley knew the way. Maybe I could make a break for Des Moines. But then, even though Riley didn't have a key, he could still get in easily. And with me gone, there'd be some action going on in my house…and it wouldn't include me.

There was no way out of it. I was stuck. Stupid Riley. Living where he isn't supposed to and giving away pets that aren't his. Oh, he was gonna get it. I'd make sure of that. I was just plotting my revenge as I pulled into the driveway.

Later tonight, I was running to the drugstore for some Nair. If I put enough in his shampoo, he'd learn that messing with me was a bad idea. The thought made me smile as I unlocked the front door to welcome Soo Jin into my home.

CHAPTER FOURTEEN

———

Hopefully, I thought as I waited for them to come in, Philby will act in such a way that Soo would feel bad about taking her kittens. I tried to communicate with my cat telepathically. Philby farted in response.

The kittens came flying from the kitchen, and soon all four cats were sitting there, lined up and staring at me. That was weird. Did I forget to feed them? I scooped up Martini. There was no way this woman was getting my Elvis look-alike.

Riley and Soo came through the door, and the woman actually squealed before getting down on her knees and pulling the remaining cats to her chest. To my complete horror, they all purred. Even Philby. Traitors.

"They're so adorable!" Soo scratched Bond and Moneypenny's heads. She looked up at me and spotted Martini. Then she looked at Philby.

Don't say it…

"Mama looks like Hitler, and that one looks like Elvis!"

Oh gee…I've never heard that before…

Riley walked past us, and I heard him opening a bottle of wine in the kitchen. I was still clutching Martini to my chest when he came back in with three glasses.

"Why did you dye your cat pink?" Soo asked as she tentatively reached out to Philby. "Did you want to match your bangs?"

It took every ounce of strength not to play Smack the Coroner.

"My Girl Scout troop played a little prank on Philby and me at a sleepover."

"Lock-in," Riley corrected. He reached to take Martini out of my arms but the look on my face must've changed his mind.

"I think Merry is very attached to Martini," he told Soo. "So she's off the table."

None of my cats should've been on the table to begin with, but how could I say that now without coming off as a total jerk?

Riley helped the doctor to her feet and led her to the couch. The two of them sat down. Where was I going to sit? It's not like I had much furniture. It had taken me a year to finally take down my Dora the Explorer sheets and put up drapes. Setting up housekeeping wasn't my thing. So I sat down on the floor, still clutching Martini.

Philby and her remaining kittens trotted over to the couch and jumped up between the two. Then they climbed onto Riley and immediately fell asleep.

"Moneypenny," Riley pointed to the girl, "and Bond," he indicated her brother, "is a boy."

Soo reached over and picked up the sleeping kittens, setting them in her lap. They didn't move. The traitors.

"Are you absolutely sure you can part with them, Merry?" Soo turned her eyes onto me.

For a moment, I thought I could get out of this. Maybe I could guilt her into leaving them. I've talked more than one person out of something they'd wanted. There was a Sherpa in Nepal—I'd convinced him that he really didn't like the snow anymore. He now lives in Florida. Yep. I'm that good.

But looking into her eager eyes and saying no would be like launching a puppy from a trebuchet into shark-infested waters. I suddenly felt bad for possibly depriving this lonely woman from some furry company.

However, these were my kittens, and I wasn't ready to give them up. Each cat had its own little quirks that I loved. For example, Moneypenny was a naughty little thing who purred when she was doing something bad—like unrolling all the toilet paper from the spool in the bathroom. Bond was the leader when it came to climbing the curtains. He started, and the girls always followed. This little boy also circled his food before eating it, as if it would explode at any moment (an excellent trait in a spy).

And Martini was my box cat. If there was a box anywhere in the house, her radar would go off, and she'd be in it before it hit the floor. I've seen her crawl into everything from a box of Girl Scout Cookies to a Milk Dud box (the latter without much success, I might add). How could I part with any of these little hellions?

"If you have any doubts," I said, "you can wait until you're ready." A date that would hopefully never come.

Soo Jin shook her head. "Oh, I couldn't take them for a couple of weeks. I'm going to paint every room before I unpack."

Riley spoke up. "Wrath could—"

This time I cut him off. "I could keep them until you're ready. Really and truly ready. There's no hurry. Take your time."

I knew what he was going to say. That bastard was going to offer me up to help the woman paint. I don't like to paint. Ever. Which is why my walls are the same color they were when I'd moved in. White. All white. If they'd been green with yellow polka dots before I moved in, they'd be green with yellow polka dots now. Actually—I'd kind of like that idea. I wonder if Kelly would do that for me.

"Great! I'll take them!" Soo sang out.

Great. Thanks Riley. You're definitely getting Nair in your shampoo now. And it wouldn't be the first time the CIA tried that. Back in the 1960s the Agency tried twice to do the same thing to Fidel Castro. One time—they were going to put a depilatory dust in his boots to make the hair in his beard fall out (things didn't work out), and another time they made a special batch of hair removing cigars (also fell through—not surprisingly). The theory was that losing his beard would psychologically affect his sense of machismo.

Obviously men came up with this plan. I think if a woman had been there, she would've asked questions along the line of...*why*? Who cares if his hair falls out? Like that would make a difference. I've never heard of a world leader who lost his mind because he'd lost his hair. And a woman wouldn't collapse if her hair fell out. She'd just use it as an opportunity to buy fancy wigs.

I was just wondering if Maria could get me the old formula for involuntary hair removal, when the doorbell rang.

"I'll get it!" I jumped to my feet, eager to get away from any conversation where I'd lose more pets and volunteer to build Soo Jin a summer home.

"Oh, hey!" I said as Kelly stood on my doorstep. "Come in."

Yes! My best friend was here, and she'd be on my side against the Riley/Soo Jin onslaught I was facing. If I'd been alone with them one minute longer I'd probably find myself massaging her feet every night before she went to bed.

"Dr. Soo Jin Body," I said as I yanked Kelly into the living room. "Meet my best friend, Kelly Roberts."

Kelly grinned and shook the coroner's hand. "You're the new medical examiner, right?"

Soo Jin looked a little confused. "Yes. That's right."

"I'm an ER nurse at the hospital," Kelly explained. "I'm on maternity leave right now, but I'll be back to work next month."

Dr. Body fluttered her eyelashes beguilingly. Ha! Good luck with that! Kelly could see through that crap. She was pretty straight-forward and didn't like messing around. This was one human Soo Jin wouldn't be able to flirt with.

"You have that beautiful baby everyone's talking about!" Soo Jin clasped her hands to her chest. "I'm so happy to meet you. I'm sure we'll be best friends."

Good luck with that, Dr. Body—Kelly already has a best friend…me. I turned to Kelly, awaiting her gloriously biting response.

"I'd love that," Kelly gushed. "I'll bring Finn by in a day or two so you can meet her!"

What. The. Hell. Where was that woman who saw through all my bluster? Where was the friend who stood back and gauged people before warming to them? Maybe Riley was right and post-pregnancy was scrambling her brains—turning her into Who's There's version of a Stepford Wife.

"Dr. Body is going to take Bond and Moneypenny," I said to Kelly, wiggling my eyebrows meaningfully.

Kelly looked from me to Soo and back to me again. "That's great!"

Not the reaction I wanted. I was kind of hoping for something along the lines of, *Oh no! How horrible! You can't take Merry's kittens! You're a monster!*

"You only need Philby and Martini," Kelly said to me with a nod.

I wanted to disagree. I wanted to ask her where my best friend had gone. And I kind of wanted to remind her that I knew things…things she wouldn't want a teenage Finn to know about. I wasn't above blackmail when necessary.

But for some reason it came out as, "Yes, I agree. I need to be responsible."

"Speaking of which," Kelly looked at me. "Do you have a moment?"

I turned to Riley and Soo. "Excuse us."

I led Kelly to my back yard, and we sat in my new glider. I loved that thing. Made of wood with some cushions I got somewhere, it was one of my favorite make out spots with Rex. Of course, I had no intention of making out with Kelly.

"You don't have to say anything!" I held my hand up as she joined me. "I totally know."

Kelly cocked her head to the side. "You do?"

I nodded, "Yes. Dr. Body is awful, and Riley offered up my kittens before I could stop him."

"What do you mean, she's awful?" Kelly frowned. "She seems pretty nice to me. And Riley is just trying to bring you to your senses. You're one cat away from becoming a crazy cat hoarder."

Okay…not quite what I'd expected her to say.

"I don't want to give up Bond and Moneypenny!" I pouted. "And Riley has no business even staying here, let alone disposing of my pets."

"That's actually what I wanted to talk to you about. Riley's here for a reason, isn't he?"

Uh-oh. Now I was stuck. Kelly had figured out what was going on in spite of Riley's post-pregnancy brain scramble theory.

"You might as well tell me now." Kelly folded her arms over her chest. Where was this version of Kelly when I'd introduced her to the sultry, cat-stealing coroner?

I took a deep breath and let it out. "He's here because of Evelyn."

Kelly's eyes narrowed to reptilian slits. "Because of Evelyn. And why would the CIA send someone here over a crazy dead woman, just because she impersonated a mother on a Girl Scout trip?"

Did she already know and just wanted to hear it from my lips? Was she bluffing? I wasn't sure. But the penalty for continuing to snowball her was high. And I needed to keep her as a friend—especially since Soo Jin was shopping for a new best friend to go with her collection of the men and kittens in my life.

"Evelyn was really Vanessa Vanderhook. And she was a CIA assassin." I flinched and opened one eye, awaiting the pummeling I was going to get.

"And?" Kelly demanded. How did she know there was more?

"And, she'd gone rogue a while back and turned traitor." There. It was out.

Kelly leaned back and closed her eyes. Either she was having a stroke or charging her batteries to let me have it. Neither option was good.

We rocked for about ten minutes without speaking. Whatever was going on in Kelly's mind—I knew one thing for sure. I was totally screwed.

Finally, I broke. "I should go get us a couple of glasses of wine…or maybe a whole bottle."

Kelly finally lifted her head and opened her eyes. She looked scary.

"Two bottles?" I asked weakly.

Kelly nodded. Oh man. I went inside hoping to hell that I actually had two bottles of wine. Maybe I should send Riley out for one hundred proof grain alcohol. I heard Riley and Soo Jin talking and laughing in the living room, but didn't join them—even though there was safety in numbers. I carried one bottle and two glasses out to the back porch and poured a healthy dose for Kelly. We drained our glasses in silence, and I poured out two more.

"How could this happen?" Kelly's voice was quiet and even. The calm before the storm?

I shrugged. "No idea. And neither Maria nor Riley had recognized her in DC."

"I'm not mad at Maria or Riley." Kelly slammed the glass of wine and held out her empty glass for a refill—which I immediately did.

"You're mad at me," I said.

Kelly sighed heavily, "No. I'm not too mad at you. And it's partly my fault for not finding more out about Evelyn before you left."

I relaxed a little but was confused. "You wouldn't have found anything. The security clearance for this intel was way beyond my pay grade. Riley only knew when they sent him back here to steal the body."

Kelly's jaw dropped—which was weird because after all this time, she shouldn't find anything shocking. "Steal the body?"

I nodded. "Yup. He just showed up on my doorstep, moved in, and demanded that I help him snatch Evelyn's corpse."

"But you didn't…" Kelly probed.

"No." I shook my head. "I'd refused. I wasn't going to hide anything from Rex anymore. So we went to see Rex, and somebody stole the body anyway."

I filled her in on what had been happening up to this point.

"So that's why Seamus died." Kelly drank the last of her wine and poured another.

"That's why Seamus was murdered," I corrected.

"What? How? Because he saw the thieves leaving town?" Kelly was turning a little green around the gills.

"That's what we think." I wasn't really sure what to say to her. This whole murder mess was getting too close to home, and it was getting personal.

"Is there anything I can do?" she asked.

This time, my jaw dropped. "What? No! You're on maternity leave, and my goddaughter needs you."

"I feel terrible." Kelly hung her head. "Poor Seamus. He didn't deserve that."

I shook my head. "No he didn't. But these are bad people. And they wanted the rest of us to know that snooping around would get us killed."

"I still want to help," Kelly insisted. "Who's There is my hometown. It's our Girl Scout troop's hometown and Finn's hometown. I don't want crap like this happening here."

"I agree with you. So would Rex and Riley. But I think the best thing you can do is stay out of it for now."

Kelly agreed, but I could see she wasn't convinced.

I changed the subject. "So, I'm going to put a depilatory in Riley's shampoo and conditioner tonight."

My best friend burst out laughing, "Why would you want that gorgeous hair to fall out?"

"I have my reasons…"

"Would one of those reasons be that stunning woman in your living room? Are you jealous that she'd go after Riley?"

I grimaced. "It's not that!" Was it? I shoved that thought aside. "It's him moving in here without even asking me and refusing to go when I demanded it. It's him giving away my pets and flirting with Dr. Body."

Kelly laughed again. "I understand. But I still think it's a little more to it than that."

I stood up, bringing my hands up to my chest. "Are you serious? I'm not into Riley. I'm into Rex. Rex and I have a future together."

"I know, but you told me when you came back from the trip that your breakup with Riley, years back, was a total misunderstanding. And I have a sneaking suspicion that's part of why he came back here."

I thought about that. It was the same sneaking suspicion I'd been having since he arrived. Was Riley trying to get me back? Ridiculous.

"He's too busy throwing himself at Soo Jin." I motioned to the house. "He's pulling out all the stops and using his best panty-melting charms."

Kelly shook her head. "He's trying to make you jealous. Duh."

"Even if that's the case…and it isn't…it won't work. So why try?"

"Because he thinks he has a chance."

"Well, if he thinks that by giving away my kittens that I'll throw myself into his arms, he can forget about it," I grumbled.

"And I like Dr. Body. You should give her a chance." Kelly stood up, and I followed her back into the house.

But I didn't want to give that woman a chance.

"Are you going so soon?" Riley stood as we walked into the living room and gave Kelly a kiss on the cheek.

Kelly nodded. "I can't be away from the baby too much."

Dr. Body held out her hand and Kelly shook it. "It's so nice to meet you. Merry has been so great—inviting me to have lunch with her, giving me her kitties. This place really is a friendly town."

I felt a little guilt twisting in my gut. Why did she have to be so nice?

Kelly raised her eyebrows at me before turning back to Soo. "She's been my best friend since we were little. I don't know what I'd do without her." And with that, she left.

Soo picked up her purse. "I should go too. I only have the one day off, and there's still so much to do." Then, to my absolute surprise, the woman hugged me. "Thanks for lunch! And thanks for the kittens!"

I watched as she walked out the door. Moneypenny and Bond ran to the door and started pawing frantically at it. Then they jumped up and climbed the curtains, and when they saw Soo get in her car, started meowing. I guess they liked her. The traitors.

CHAPTER FIFTEEN

I filled Riley in on the reason for Kelly's visit.

"That's great of her to volunteer to help," Riley said. "But you're right to tell her she can't. These people are dangerous. And my goddaughter needs her mother."

"That's what I said," I grumbled. It sounded so much better coming from Riley.

"Hey, thanks for giving away my animals…" I grouched.

Riley looked surprised. "What? You were actually going to keep all four?"

"I don't know! I hadn't thought about it! But it was my decision to make. Not yours. And not just because some drop-dead gorgeous medical examiner bats her eyelash extensions at you."

He studied me for a moment. "Sorry about that. But I do think it's the right thing. Not only are two cats far more manageable, but it gets us into the doctor's good graces."

"That was about leverage?" I couldn't believe it.

"Half of it was. Remember, Soo Jin is the only person still living who's seen our killer couple."

A wash of cold fear flushed over me. "You think she's next on their list."

He nodded. "I talked to Rex about this. He's going to keep an eye on her."

"When did you talk to Rex?" I sputtered.

"While you were outside with Kelly. I told Soo Jin that she should keep on her guard and gave her my number. Then I called Rex and he agreed to post an officer outside her house. Ted Dooley at the hospital is going to put one of his security guys on her when she's at work."

I stared at him as if he'd sprouted two heads. "You did all that while I was outside with Kelly."

Riley looked surprised. "It's standard operating procedure, Wrath."

He was right. And grudgingly, I had to admit he did the right thing.

"Do you think they'll really go after Dr. Body?" I asked.

"I don't know for sure, but it seems pretty likely."

"Was Soo Jin worried when you told her?" She was a civilian after all—not really used to the situations Riley and I were.

"Not too much. Did you know she has a black belt in Aikido?" Riley walked into the kitchen, and seeing the empty wine bottle on the counter, gave me a questioning look.

"That makes me feel a little better…" I said as I washed out the wine glasses. "I guess we should let Rex do his thing. Then we can do our thing."

Riley gave me a slightly slutty smile. "And what's our thing?"

Huh. Maybe Kelly was right. A little.

"Our thing is to find these bastards before they kill anyone else in my town," I answered.

Was I mistaken, or did Riley look a little disappointed? "I'm going to call the Agency and see if they've found out anything more." He walked down the hall to his bedroom and closed the door behind him.

That man was so frustrating! He confused me in every way possible. I needed some air. Grabbing my keys, I picked up Philby and headed to my car.

When I was worked up or upset, I drove around town. One time a month ago, I took Philby. She loved it. Maybe she needed a break from her kittens. Maybe she had a thing for cars. Whatever the reason, I backed out of the driveway with my cat sticking her head out of the passenger window.

Don't worry—I'd devised a little safety harness so she couldn't jump out. Philby acted like a dog with the wind whipping across her face. Her tail switched back and forth violently as we went. It looked like she had the right idea, so I opened my window too and felt the late afternoon breezes wash over me.

We started out driving on Main Street. Normally, I loved driving around, feeling invisible. But too late I forgot that would be impossible on this trip. Why? Because I had a neon pink cat hanging out of the window.

People stopped what they were doing and stood staring, jaws on the ground, at the bright pink Hitler cat hanging out of my window. What was I thinking? I'd just wanted to get away from it all, but "it all" was staring nonstop at me. I guess I'd gotten so used to my cat this color that I just assumed no one would notice.

I was wrong. No…scratch that…I was the wrongest wrong that I could be. Things got worse when I passed a bunch of teenagers and they immediately took out their cell phones and started snapping pictures. I could just imagine the caption on Facebook or Instagram: *Crazy Cat Hoarder Dyes Cats Pink*. Or, if we were lucky, we'd probably make the *National Enquirer* with some trumped up story about alien cats living in small-town Iowa.

I tried to pull Philby back down onto the seat, but she was having none of it. This was her "me" time, and how dare I try to take that away from her. Instead, I veered off of Main onto a quiet side street, making my way to the outer limits of town. When your pink cat parade doesn't work, try country roads.

When I turned sixteen and got my driver's license, I did what all other teenagers do. I drove from one end of town to the other. That took about ten minutes, so I'd do a circuit loop which added about twenty. Mom hated sending me to the store for something because I'd get it, and then drive around for half an hour, making dinner late.

That's when I'd discovered country roads. Sure, they were mostly gravel, which led to some pretty hair-raising fishtailing. But it was quiet. Peaceful. And beautiful. Yes, you heard me right. Beautiful.

There was nothing like driving alone on a road where you could see for fifteen miles in all directions. A green sea of corn stalks swayed in the breezes, and the ditches were full of bright orange lilies. Redwing blackbirds sat on fence posts every fifty feet or so, guarding their territory, and now and then you could spot a hawk circling lazily in the sky. If no one needed me home, I'd drive for hours, learning every back road around Who's There.

So that's where I headed. Out there, no one would notice my cat. Well, except for a hawk or two who'd probably think they'd hit the jackpot since their food practically glowed in the dark. Dusk was settling in, so we might come upon a deer or two.

As the tires hit gravel, my whole being relaxed. I hadn't done this in years. I wondered why. I've been here for almost two years and hadn't even thought of doing it.

Philby seemed a little less thrilled. Maybe she preferred the snapchatting kids or she loved the attention. And then, she spotted the blackbirds. This was better because her food wasn't moving. Of course, she had no access to it, but still, she could give the stink eye to a different bird every minute. And there'd always be another one and another one and another one.

I switched on the headlights and drove slowly, randomly turning right and left onto deserted roads. It was heaven. Pure heaven. Philby's tail switched violently as she started chattering at the birds we passed. I'm pretty sure they weren't intimidated.

About three miles outside of town, I turned right to find an old, decaying farmhouse with a crumbling barn. This was the old Philips' place, even though it was abandoned long before I was born. Rumor was, when I was in high school, this was where most underage kegger parties were held. I say '"rumor" because I wasn't popular enough to be invited to said parties. Not that I minded. Okay, I minded. A little.

I turned off my lights and pulled over on the shoulder. The house was a Victorian with lots of embellishments. It must've been beautiful at one time. But now the paint had peeled off down to the natural wood. Windows were broken long ago, and the roof sagged. It wasn't creepy. It was sad to see the house in such disrepair.

Word was the Philips family had moved into town in the 1970s. They still owned the land out here and farmed a great deal of it, but the original buildings were allowed to fall apart. I unbuckled my seat belt to move closer to the passenger window for a better view. The sky's color ranged to one matching my cat and faded into a deep violet.

For a moment, I entertained the idea of buying this lot and fixing up the place. Bring it back to its original glory. But then, what would I do with it? I guess I could farm Riley out here when he showed up, maybe turn it into a bed and breakfast for the CIA.

Riley. Kelly thought he came here to see me, more than to steal a body. We had a past. A very romantic one—that was shattered when I caught him holding another woman. I dumped him immediately. But recently it turned out that I'd been mistaken. The whole thing had been a mistake. A mistake Riley seriously regretted.

Was he back here to woo me? Did I want him to woo me?

Oh for crying out loud, Wrath! You have Rex now. And Rex lives here—he's not in the CIA and won't ever disappear for months at a time. Riley is over. We're just friends. Just because he keeps barging into my life doesn't mean I have to be with him.

Ugh! Why does everything have to be so complicated? Maybe Riley flirting with Soo Jin wasn't a bad thing. Maybe it's just what I need. Yes! That's the answer! I'll encourage the two of them. And then I don't have to worry about her and Rex.

Rex. That man was amazing. Handsome, funny, sexy, smart—he was everything a woman could ever want. And I loved him. And he loved me. He also loved my cats. The man made my stomach flutter, and sometimes being around him made me feel like I was gasping for air.

I leaned back in my seat, feeling much better. It's amazing what some fresh air, a pink cat, and a drive in the country can do. Now it was time to go back. Maybe I'd pick up some fried chicken. Riley had never had Whitey's Chicken. It was the best in the whole state. And it was made and sold in a gas station.

With a new sense of purpose, I reached to turn the key in the ignition. And that's when I saw it.

A couple of average height and brown hair appeared in the doorway of the house and walked to the dilapidated barn. I heard an engine rev before a white pickup truck drove out of the barn. I started the engine but kept the lights off, backing down the road as fast as I could. In the dim light, they wouldn't notice the plume of dust that usually telegraphed the presence of another car.

Backing up instead of going forward would hide me for a moment, but that's about all. Backing up on a dark road with no lights and turning left at the same time was quite a challenge, and I managed it just as the nose of the truck came into view.

My heart was pounding as I spotted a culvert over a ditch that led into a cornfield. These were little driveways for farmers who wanted to check their crops. I backed in over the culvert and as far into the field as I could without destroying the corn stalks. Once I was enclosed on three sides, I turned the car off and, grabbing an irritated Philby, dove for the floor.

The rumbling engine was getting closer. Damn. I'd hoped they'd turn right onto the road and I'd avoid them completely. Maybe they wouldn't see us. It was very dark now, and their headlights wouldn't sweep my car. I hunkered down and waited.

The truck engine moved past my position so slowly I thought my heart would stop. I thought about defending myself, but all I had readily at hand was a grumpy pink cat and my cell phone. I'd only grabbed my wallet when I fled the house earlier.

In any other instance, I could take them. But there were two people. And if they were who I thought they were, they were well armed. I'd have to rely on either running them over or escaping through the field.

The engine told me the truck was right in front of my car. I held my breath. Philby didn't even fidget. She seemed to know this wasn't a good time. Smart cat. At last, the engine noise faded away, and I exhaled. I still waited a few more minutes, just to make sure, before sitting back up.

They were headed back toward town. I'd have to go the other way, past the old Philips' place, in order to get to town unnoticed. I started the engine but kept the lights off. After creeping forward and seeing no one, I turned left onto the road and took a right onto the road past the abandoned house.

I paused as I started to pass the house. Doing a little math in my head, I figured I had at least twenty minutes before the earliest time they could return. I pulled off the road and drove the car around to the back of the house, but out of sight of the barn, and got out of the car. Philby pawed at the windows as I rolled them up, but she was staying here. I turned on the flashlight app on my phone and sprinted to the house.

Very gently I stepped onto the porch. It was a miracle that the rotting boards held my weight. The door was wide open, and I slipped inside. The house was in better shape here, but I didn't have much time to take in the view. Working quickly, I searched each room in the old house. Someone was definitely living here. I found evidence of food, footprints in the dust, and an inflatable mattress with a pillow and blanket.

I paused at the foot of the staircase. Did I have time? I decided I did, and keeping to the outside of each step, tried to race up to the next floor. At one point a board groaned beneath me, but eventually I made it to the top. These old houses had very steep, very narrow stairs. The heat on the second floor was stifling. So was the smell. Something had died here.

There were only two rooms, and the first room was completely empty. It was the second room where I found it. There, sitting on the floor, was a body bag. I unzipped one end of it, wondering why the hell I was doing that. Brown hair. I recognized that hair.

A flash of light hit the window and I dropped flat on the floor. I heard a vehicle pulling up under the windows. Damn. I'd cut it too close. I looked down at the body.

"Well, Evelyn, this is a fine spot you've gotten me into."

"I said I'd get it!" a man's voice shouted outside.

"You shouldn't have forgotten it in the first place, idiot!" a woman hissed back.

It was them. The people who took Evelyn's body. The people who'd killed Seamus Bailey. I'd found them, unfortunately. And pretty soon…they'd find me.

CHAPTER SIXTEEN

———

I heard someone walk through the front doorway.

"Dammit, Red!" the man shouted. "You left the door open!"

The woman's voice fired back from outside, "What are you worried about? Afraid someone will break in?" She snorted.

"No, you moron!" the man said. "I'm worried that coyotes or cougars will get that body!"

Red said nothing. The guy was right. We still had coyotes, and even though very rare, cougars were sighted every now and then. I was still crouched under the window in the same room as Evelyn's corpse. I pulled out my cell and sent out a text message. Then I prayed because there wasn't much else I could do.

The door slammed below, and I heard footsteps downstairs. The woman must've come inside. What had they forgotten? Hopefully not the body. Of course, if the guy had forgotten something that big, you'd think this Red would've noticed.

My phone buzzed, and I glanced briefly at the reply before shutting off the phone. No point in the light giving me away. Looking around the room, there wasn't much I could use as a weapon if they came upstairs. Worse yet, Philby was trapped in my car—a car that could be discovered at any second. How did I get myself into these situations?

Minutes passed as I heard the couple rooting around on the first level. I prayed that they'd find what they were looking for and leave—preferably without noticing the strange car with the pink cat out back.

"How could you lose the silencer?" Red shrieked.

"I don't know!" the man shot back. He sounded very angry.

"Dammit, Blue! I should've brought it myself," the woman snarled.

Red was the woman? And the man's name was Blue? Either they were named by a crayon maker or these were code names. I'd heard worse. Once, in Finland, I'd worked with a couple who called themselves Pickled and Herring.

How much time had passed? Maybe ten minutes? It sounded like they were taking the house apart board by board. Something caught my eye in the corner of the room. Damn. It was the silencer. And sooner or later, they'd come upstairs to find it.

"This is all your fault!" The woman shouted. "All of it!"

The man fired back, "It's your fault Vanessa skipped out with the puzzle box! You were supposed to be watching her!"

Vanessa—oh right. That was Evelyn's real name. So whoever these two were, they knew who and what she was. Hmmm…both had American accents. Not a foreign terrorist group. Domestic terrorists? That was worse. That was too close to home. And what was this box they were talking about?

Most importantly, they were looking for a missing silencer. You don't carry one with you unless you're planning to use it. That was very bad news.

I had an idea what they'd planned to do with it. Take out the only person still living who could identify them. Soo Jin Body. Somehow, I had to make sure they didn't find me and didn't kill her.

"I'll check upstairs," Blue, the guy, said.

The room was dark, and I couldn't see a light fixture or anything that would illuminate me. As Blue started stomping up the stairs, I risked a glance out the window, hoping I'd have a ledge or part of the roof to step out onto. No such luck. The drop from the window to the ground was devastating. I'd survive, but I'd definitely break something.

Blue reached the top of the stairs, and I heard him head into the first room. Very slowly, I started to creep, on all fours, toward the space behind the door. It was dark there, and if I was discovered, at least I'd have the drop on him.

"Find it?" Red shrieked from the first floor.

"Not yet!" Blue snarled.

He was coming out of the other room and making his way toward the silencer, Evelyn's body, and me. The good news was that I could definitely take him by surprise and probably render him unconscious. The bad news was that any scuffle upstairs was bound to be heard downstairs. And at least one of them was most likely armed.

I flattened myself against the wall, behind the door, trying desperately not to breathe. In spite of the darkness, a shadow loomed over the threshold and into the room. If he took two more steps, I'd have to act. And then Red would come flying up those stairs.

No matter how many times I've been in situations like these, it was still pretty terrifying. You don't get used to it with time or experience. The pounding of my heart gave that away. You know how in movies, the dashing, dapper spy gleefully throws himself in harm's way without another thought? Well that's just an absurd fantasy from Hollywood. I didn't know of one single spy, on any side, who wasn't nervous about a confrontation.

Blue took one step inside the room. I could see a profile through the crack between the door and its frame. He was about my height and a bit heavier than me, and I knew I could take him down if I had to. Which I didn't want to do. I saw as he reached behind him. Oh great. He has a gun. That just added to the insanity of jumping him.

Click. A beam started sweeping the room from right to left. I would've sighed with relief, except that it meant he'd be able to see me soon. I pressed myself hard against the wall behind me, ready to push off and launch, hitting him with the door. If I got lucky, I'd have two or three seconds to disarm him before he'd realize what was happening. If I was lucky.

A sound wailed in the distance, and I relaxed a little. Rex. He got my text message.

"That's a siren!" Red yelled. "We've got to go now!"

Blue vanished from the doorway and ran down the hallway and down the stairs. I heard two sets of footsteps echoing through the first floor and heard the door slam shut. In seconds the truck's engine roared to life and raced off to the gravel road and away from the house.

I waited a moment before turning my cell back on and using the flashlight to negotiate the stairs. The siren got closer. It would be here soon. But these stairs were tough to navigate, so I took my time.

The squad car roared up to the front door just as I walked outside. Rex stepped out, gun drawn. When he spotted me waving like an idiot, he relaxed and moved to the back of the car and opened the door.

"You shouldn't take chances like this!" Kelly cried as she hurled herself into my arms.

I extracted myself. "I'm glad you got the message."

"If you hadn't texted and mentioned the old Philips' place and told me to bring Rex and a squad car with sirens blazing, you might be dead now!" She hugged me once again. I hugged her back. It seemed like the thing to do.

"That was good thinking," Rex said as he stepped up and hugged both of us.

I pulled away, "I thought the sound of a siren would scare them off. Thanks."

Rex shook his head as if he found it hard to believe I'd put myself in danger…again.

"You'll need a team to process this place. It's where the killers have been hiding out. Evelyn's upstairs," I said as I walked around the side of the house to my car.

Philby glared daggers at me until I opened the door and took her out. Apparently she wasn't keen on spy work.

Half an hour later the whole place was being gone over with a fine-tooth comb. The body was carried out and placed in the back of an ambulance (the presence of which confused me as the body was…well…a dead body), and Kevin was carrying out a baggie with the silencer in it.

"Red and Blue?" Riley said. He'd shown up a few minutes after Rex. Kelly had given him directions. "I'll send those names through the database at Langley and see what they have."

"Ms. Wrath," Rex called out from the direction of the barn. "Could you come over here, please?"

Riley and I walked into the barn, which was now lit up like Christmas.

"Oh no," I gasped. In the middle of the room was a long table. The table was groaning under the weight of blocks of C-4. The stuff you would use to make a bomb. Or in this case, enough to blow up four city blocks in Chicago.

"This isn't good," Riley said.

Rex called the Sheriff's department and the Iowa State Police. This was going to take all three agencies to deal with this much material. Riley and I left him to do his job.

The police didn't find much else. There were no telltale wallets or even a resume for Red or Blue. Okay, so I know it's ridiculous to think they were that stupid, but a girl can dream, can't she? It was after midnight before we were done and driving back to town in a weird convoy led by a pink cat.

Rex made sure I pulled into my drive before taking off to get Kelly home. Riley followed me into the house. Philby jumped out of my arms the moment we'd cleared the threshold. She passed her three confused kittens and raced off to the kitchen. Apparently, she was more hungry than ready for a family reunion.

I followed her into the kitchen and took out a bottle of wine with two glasses. By the time I got back to the living room, Riley was on both his laptop and cell, telling someone about Red and Blue. It gave me a moment to think.

According to what they'd said back at the old Philips' place, Red was responsible for Vanessa slipping away with some box. They were here to find her and it. Whatever it was. And then a lightbulb switched on in my brain. I picked up my phone and dialed.

"Hello?" Lauren's voice answered on the second ring.

"Hey Lauren, it's Ms. Wrath," I said. Riley gave me a puzzled look but said nothing.

"Mrs. Wrath?" the girl asked.

No matter how many times I'd asked them in the entire history of our troop, the girls never called me Ms., only Mrs. I'd given up on arguing with them long ago.

"That's right, it's me," I said. "I have to ask you a question."

There was a moment of silence, "Well, okay. But I'm s'posed to be getting ready for bed."

"It's about the puzzle box," I said, noting a sharp intake of air on the other end. "You didn't just find it in your bag at the church, did you?"

"I can't talk about it," Lauren hesitated.

"You can talk to me about it. Remember when we had that workshop on trusted adults? Well, I am one."

Riley stifled a snicker, and I glared at him.

"I don't know…" she said slowly.

"What if I told you it's important? For a spy case?"

"Really?" Lauren's attitude changed. "Like a life and death situation? Something like that?"

I nodded, even though I knew she couldn't see me. "That's exactly right."

"Well…" the child said. "I guess it's okay then."

I waited. Nothing. Remember what I said about being very literal with the girls?

"So?"

"That woman gave it to me. She told me to hide it," Lauren said very matter-of-factly.

"What woman?" A glimmer of light started to come on in my brain.

"The one who went on the trip with us. The one we didn't know."

"Mrs. Trout? You saw Mrs. Trout at the church?" I asked.

Riley's eyes grew wide. He put down his cell and closed his laptop as he leaned forward. I switched the call to speakerphone. I'd have to tell him what she said anyway.

"I went to the bathroom alone. I didn't take a buddy, like you told us to."

"That's all right, kiddo," I said. "Your moms were there, so I didn't insist you use the buddy system."

"She was in the bathroom. She looked a little freaked out," Lauren continued. "She handed me the box and asked me to hide it for her. Then she ran out of the bathroom."

Well that explained where the box had come from.

"Why didn't you tell me?" I asked.

"Because I didn't do the buddy system, and it was stranger danger. I didn't want to get in trouble." I felt like I could see her standing there, a finger in her mouth, a worried look on her face.

"I'm glad you told me now." I'd decided to cut her some slack. None of this was her fault.

Riley got up and left the living room. He returned seconds later with the box.

"Okay," Lauren said, and hung up. Our call was over.

Riley used the sequence to open the box. He took the black pouch out and dumped the SD card into his hand.

"It's not that," I said. "That's a red herring."

Riley's right eyebrow arched. "To throw us off track?"

I nodded. "To keep us from looking for the really important thing."

Taking the box from him, I ran my fingers over the black velvet lining until I felt a bump. A bump that shouldn't have been there. Riley handed me a pocketknife I didn't know he had, and I pried up one corner of the fabric, pulling it back until whatever was in there was exposed.

"It's a folded up piece of paper," I said as I eased it open.

I was wrong. It was a photo of Red and Blue, looking at a map on a table. Written in the upper right hand corner, someone had written G 11 W.

"At least we have a better look at those two." Riley smoothed the photo and took a picture of it with his phone. He was sending it to Langley for further study.

"What's wrong?" Riley searched my face.

Everything was wrong. "The map," I said, pointing to it.

Riley frowned and squinted. It was kind of hard to see, since it was flat on the table in the photo. But I knew where it was.

"It's Willow Grove, Iowa," I said as I reached under the coffee table and brought out the atlas. I opened it to the right page and pointed. "G," I pointed to the top of the map, "And 11," I pointed to the side. Very slowly I brought my right finger down while my left finger slid sideways until they met at Willow Grove.

"That's only ten miles from here," Riley said. "What's so significant about Willow Grove?"

"Nothing. Believe me. It's only a couple thousand people. It's what's going to be there that's important."

"What do you mean?"

"Remember the news from the other night? The president of the United States is going to be there tomorrow. He's doing a campaign stop at the fertilizer plant there."

"Oh no." Riley finally grasped the situation.

I nodded, "Oh yes. Whoever they're with, and if they have more explosives, Red and Blue are going to blow up that fertilizer plant with the leader of the free world inside." And it looked like it was going to happen in just twelve hours.

CHAPTER SEVENTEEN

———

Riley was immediately on the phone with the CIA while I called the Secret Service office in Omaha. They were the closest office, which meant they were on the ground there now.

I was transferred to Agent Bill Savage, the officer already in Willow Grove. After explaining what we'd found out about a possible attack, he replied in a tone normally reserved for an incontinent, lobotomized Communist.

"We've checked the plant, and everything's fine, Ms. Wrath," he grumped.

Translation—*we don't like the CIA, and stop acting smarter than us or we will tell on you.*

"Check again," I insisted. "Because what we've found could mean an assassination attempt on POTUS."

POTUS is a fancy acronym for President of the United States. What's funny is that the Secret Service thinks that's a secret code. But I found out about it watching *The West Wing* on TV back in the 1990s. And the creativity stopped there, folks, because the First Lady is FLOTUS, and they even call the Supreme Court SCOTUS. Lazy, lazy Secret Service.

Now that I thought of it—most government agencies used acronyms. There's CIA for Central Intelligence Agency, FBI for Federal Bureau of Investigation, and even CDC for Centers for Disease Control and Prevention. Wait…shouldn't that be CDCAP? Seems like someone dropped the ball on that one.

I heard mumbling in the background and went back to paying attention. Agent Savage—which, by the way, is an awesome name—was arguing with someone. Riley looked questioningly at me while he was on his phone. I rolled my eyes, which told him pretty much how it was going.

"I think this is bullshit," Savage growled. "But bring what you've got over here, and I'll at least take a look at it."

I knew he'd give in. No one, especially an agent from Omaha, wanted to see the president and half the town of Willow Grove, Iowa blow up just because they didn't check all the doors and windows.

I hung up just as Riley did and filled him in on what was happening.

"Yeah, the Agency wants us to check it out. I guess we're going on a little road trip."

"You have no idea. Little road trip is right. It'll take us about ten minutes to get there," I said.

And it would. Unless Riley drove like my grandmother and kept it under forty-one miles an hour. But come to think of it—she never once got in an accident. Of course, she was half-blind and cheated on her eye exam, so maybe she thought she was doing sixty. It's hard to say.

After putting out some food for the cats, we got into Riley's SUV. I called Rex from the road to explain what was going on. He didn't sound happy either. All the men in my immediate vicinity seemed to think this was my fault…which seemed pretty unfair.

"Hit the drive-through," I demanded as we came up to a fast-food joint.

To my complete surprise, Riley did as I asked. Mr. Health Weirdo ordered a salad while I got the deluxe burger with fries and a chocolate shake. We pulled back onto the road, and I dug in. Riley kept glancing over at my food.

"Hungry?" I asked before shoving a fistful of french fries into my mouth.

"I'll wait for my salad, thanks." Riley focused on the road, but more than once I saw him side-eying my dinner.

"You'll have to, because you ordered a salad. Not exactly finger food." Who the hell orders a salad when there are so many other wonderfully greasy options? That makes no sense.

We arrived in Willow Grove before he had a chance to reply. In spite of the late hour, this sleepy little town was buzzing with activity, because here, two cars on Main Street is practically a traffic jam. I'd always liked Willow Grove. It looked like Disneyland's Main Street USA with its cute little brick ice cream shop, theatre, and town hall. This town had a building code that all new construction had to be ridiculously adorable. Even the gas stations were red brick with black shutters. You had to love that.

The fertilizer plant was on the other side of town and surrounded with news vans by the time we got there. This building, unlike the rest of the town aesthetic, just looked like a factory. I guess even Willow Grove couldn't think of a way to make a manure manufacturing building adorable.

We drove up to a man in a suit who was guarding the entrance. Savage had already marked us as "okay," whatever that meant. I was a tad wounded he didn't label us "exceptional," but there is a bit of a rivalry between the two agencies. Okay, there's a huge rivalry. These two organizations did not like each other.

Riley parked the car and reached for his salad as I crumpled up my wrappers and tossed them on the floor and jumped out. I guess seeing and smelling my food made him a little ravenous, because I've never seen anyone attack plastic and Styrofoam with such violence.

"Ms. Wrath? Mr. Andrews?" A very short, hostile man in a cheap suit approached. "Bill Savage. Let's get this over with."

Riley was in the process of taking his first bite. He put the spork back down with a sigh and got out of the van. By the way—I love sporks. You'd think that with their spoony shape and tiny fork tines that they'd be fairly safe, right? Well, you'd be wrong because one time in Vladivostok I used a spork to kill a Chechen terrorist. I would've used it on his partner, but the damn thing broke, and I didn't have a spare. So, I had to use my firearm, but that wasn't as much fun.

Savage frowned as he glimpsed the salad on Riley's seat when he opened the door.

"A salad? You'd never last long in the Secret Service on that crap. You need calories, man."

Why did men call each other "man"? That never made sense to me. Kelly's never called me "woman," and I've never called Philby "cat." Do they do it to remind themselves what gender they are? You'd think they wouldn't forget something like that, but who knows?

I shrugged, "I told him that, but he wouldn't listen."

Riley shot me a look, but I ignored him. "I wouldn't even attempt to join the Secret Service because I have something called *dignity*."

Savage's neck turned purple, but he wisely didn't respond. Instead, he turned to me.

"What's wrong with your hair, Ms. Wrath?" Savage pointed as if I'd somehow forgotten where my hair was. Oh right. The pink bangs.

"That's not regulation!" he barked. I caught Riley trying not to grin. "You should have respect for the office, Wrath!"

"Actually this is part of my disguise," I sniffed. "I'm undercover in an all-female, Iowa-based terrorist ring." I didn't think my Girl Scout troop would mind me referring to them as terrorists. In fact, they'd probably like it.

I was just about to follow up with a joke—how many Secret Service agents does it take to screw in a lightbulb? The answer varies based on who the president is, but I assure you— it's hilarious. Unfortunately, I was rudely interrupted.

"Do you think this is funny?" Savage shouted as if we weren't a few feet away. "I don't have time for this! What is this so called evidence you *think* you have?"

I decided not to go for the cheap shot, even though I could have. It's no secret that the Service is the lowest ranked team in the Homeland Security softball league (the CIA is first, by the way, but that's probably because they cheat). Instead, I handed the photo to the diminutive agent and explained why we thought tomorrow's event was a target. It was kind of hard talking to him because he was a whole head shorter than me.

He frowned. "I think that's a pretty flimsy theory." Savage handed me back the photo.

"You can't be serious," I said. "There's a potential threat aimed at Willow Grove. And tomorrow is the only time anything important will ever happen here."

That wasn't entirely true. Once, in the '90s, a bunch of Iowa state legislators were caught in a tavern in Willow Grove, throwing a private party with a bunch of call girls and a donkey. It made the national news for like…a minute. I always wondered where they got those prostitutes from. Probably from Sin City, aka Omaha. The donkey was probably local.

Bill Savage grimaced as if he smelled something bad. I'd bet it was Riley's vinaigrette dressing, but said nothing.

"At least walk us through the plant," Riley said calmly.

It's an old spy trick. When someone starts screaming, you speak softly so they have to stop screaming to listen. It works every time.

"Then we can tell Langley and Senator Czrygy that you'd done your job."

I tried not to laugh out loud. Riley had just mentioned my dad—who chaired the Senate Committee on Homeland Security and Governmental Affairs and was one of our Iowa senators. Savage didn't know that Czrygy was my father.

"Fine," the man snapped. "But you're taking precious time away from us setting up."

Oh right…we were impeding *him* doing *his* job. Well he won't have a job tomorrow if the president explodes in a fecal factory.

We followed him into the main entrance. Savage took us through every office in the administrative wing. Outside of a few seed corn calendars and various John Deere memorabilia, there wasn't much to see. Then we stepped out onto the main floor.

There must've been a hundred men and a few women racing in every direction. Some were in suits, like the Secret Service agent we were standing over, and the rest were dressed in everything from flannel shirts and jeans to khakis and polo shirts. It was a total mess. No organization at all. How did they think they could keep this place clear?

"We've been over every inch of this building in the last four days," Savage said. "Every single employee has had background checks. Hell, the whole town has had background checks. So I don't see how there could be any threat."

Seriously? "The threat won't come from someone who lives in Willow Grove, or even Iowa. You can't prescreen people you don't know—and that's where the problem lies," I insisted.

Riley nodded. "She's right. There are too many people. Do you know who all of them are? Seems to me it would be very easy for a terrorist to infiltrate this mess."

Savage turned beet red. "I know how to do my job! No one who wasn't prescreened will come anywhere close to this plant tomorrow!"

The little man had had enough of our meddling. He escorted us back to the parking lot, ignoring our protests. We got back into the car, and Savage walked away. The Secret Service was done with us.

We didn't drive off right away. Riley was attacking his now wilted salad. I found a couple of loose french fries in the bag and devoured them. They were cold but still better than any salad.

"Now what?" Riley asked as he wiped his face on a napkin.

"Now," I said as I took out my cell, "I call Dad. I hope you packed a suit, because we will be coming back here tomorrow as part of Senator Michael Czrygy's team."

Of course, my father was only too happy to have us there. "I wasn't going to go," he told me on the phone. "But now it looks like it could be fun!"

Only my dad would think a possible terrorist act in a fertilizer plant would be fun.

"Are you in Des Moines?" I asked. If he was, I'd be upset with him for not telling me in advance. I'd wanted him to meet Philby and the kittens.

"No," Dad said. "But I will be there in the morning."

Since Who's There was the nearest city to Willow Grove, it made sense he'd book a hotel in my town. I couldn't have him over because *someone* was squatting in my guest room. So, if we got lucky and didn't have an explosion, I'd get to have Dad over for dinner. Then he'd meet my cats. Well, for as long as I still had four, that is.

We made arrangements to pick up my father at the Radisson in the morning and drive him to Willow Grove. I'd offered to pick him up at the airport, but he declined. I didn't ask.

It was probably some super-secret Illuminati carpool or something.

I sat in the kitchen in my pajamas with a glass of wine and Martini in my lap. Riley was making calls from his room. His room? Man, we seriously needed to straighten this out. The idea that Riley had his own room in *my* house had taken root now. I didn't like it.

To be honest, I was having trouble even thinking about sleep. Terrorism, whether domestic or foreign, was nothing to take lightly. I'd had enough of that back in my spy days. That's why I'd come back to Iowa, to get away from it.

But now the fight was coming here. Which sucked. This was my home. I had a personal connection to Who's There and its people. Seamus Bailey had been murdered. Bad guys had taken up residence in the old Philips' place. And Lucinda wasn't on fire any more. That was the real threat, if you asked me.

All kidding aside, in the past two years I'd set up a home with pets, a best friend, a boyfriend, and twelve little girls who thought I was amazing. Okay…they never said out loud that they thought I was amazing—that's just a given at this point.

I'd lived in maybe a dozen different countries over my career as a secret agent. For the most part, they'd all been exotic, fascinating, and dangerous. And as much fun as that was, the best years have all been here, in the small town I'd grown up in. If you'd asked me if I'd thought that possible five years ago, I would've laughed.

I wasn't laughing now. At all. Red and Blue or whoever they were and Evelyn aka Vanessa did not belong here. Tomorrow, I was going to take them down, no matter what it took. And then, I'd have to figure out a way to keep bad guys away from home in the future.

The idea of Riley moving here had been bothering me. Probably because I realized he was somewhat seriously considering it. For a spy, settling down was like being reincarnated in the same place for fifteen consecutive lifetimes.

If I was a magnet for trouble, I can only imagine that two of us would be worse. But then, there'd be two of us to ward things off too. Did I want him here? No. He would just complicate things. This weird unfinished romantic mess wouldn't have any kind of closure—especially if he moved next door. Although the way things were going, Riley probably thought he'd already moved into my house.

He knew my troop. He and Kelly were friends, and Riley was Finn's godfather. What about Rex? My boyfriend had never said anything bad about Riley and always behaved professionally toward him. But how did he really feel about my ex being here so much and living in my house to boot?

I shook my head and gave up. Besides, I needed to get some sleep—tomorrow would be a dangerous day. I headed down the hallway, the four cats leading me in the procession. Outside of Riley's room, Moneypenny and Bond began clawing at his door. I could hear him on the phone, and without breaking his conversation, he opened the door and let the kittens in.

Philby and Martini had the good grace to join me in my room. After washing my face and brushing my teeth, I crawled into bed and eventually, willed myself to sleep.

CHAPTER EIGHTEEN

———

I awoke to find two cats standing over my head, looking down into my face. Light streamed through the blinds, and I sat up. Philby and Martini began yowling loudly at the door. Riley was probably already up and had fed the other two cats. A devious and deeply unfair thing to do when the other cats were trapped in my room.

I let them out, closing the door behind them. After a quick shower, I dressed into the lone suit in my closet and met up with the rest of the household in the kitchen. Once more I'd tried to wash the pink out of my hair, and once more I was unable to do so. It would have to do, even though I might look a tad unbelievable as a member of Dad's staff. Oh well.

Riley was making pancakes and dressed immaculately in a dark gray suit, light gray shirt, and red tie. I could smell his aftershave from the breakfast bar. He looked great and smelled wonderful. But then, when didn't he?

"I would've let Philby and Martini out, but I thought you'd like your privacy," Riley said as he put some pancakes on a plate in front of me.

"I think you've made enemies for life," I answered as I picked up a fork.

Philby was sitting at Riley's feet, glaring menacingly. I was pretty sure she could take him. Riley reached down and scratched between her ears, and she gave up being angry and resorted to purring. So fickle.

"Big day today," I said as I buttered my pancakes. They were the perfect consistency of light and fluffy. The bastard.

Riley nodded as he put some on his plate and sat down to eat. "The Agency wants me to apprehend Red and Blue."

"Of course," I said. "I want that too."

He shook his head. "No, the Agency wants me to be the *only* one who apprehends them. They don't want these two falling into any other government organization's hands."

I sighed. "I love it when they give out an impossible task. What am I saying—they're always impossible."

He shook his head. "Not impossible. We can do this."

"In the middle of hundreds of people, including the Secret Service and State Police?"

"Why not?" Riley picked up his keys. "We've got to go."

I stifled a yawn. This was exhausting. Saving the world made me tired. Okay, so not the whole world—just my corner of it. I rinsed my plate and dumped it in the sink—earning a look of horror from Riley. Oh well. He'd have to deal with it.

"Senator!" I called out as Dad walked toward me in the lobby of his hotel.

I wanted to throw my arms around him, but that would draw curious looks. You had to be careful when your father is a public figure. Once, when I'd come home for summer break and Dad was just a state congressman, we went out to the Catfish Farm for dinner with some friends of my parents. The wait was long, so Dad and I offered to go fetch drinks from the bar. As we approached, a group of middle-aged women sitting at the bar, and all made up as if they seriously misunderstood how makeup worked, turned to stare.

After a few seconds, one of the women gave me a stern glare and said, "Honey, Congressman Czrygy is old enough to be your father."

The other painted ladies nodded as if they'd busted the legislator with a very young woman. And they'd be only too happy to spread the word all over town before we even got home.

"Honey," I said in my sugariest voice, "He *is* my father."

The women immediately changed their tune and started flirting with Dad. Aren't people idiots sometimes?

Leslie Langtry | 158

"Ms. Wrath, Mr. Andrews." Senator Michael Czrygy nodded, slipping in a wink. If he was startled by my pink bangs, he didn't say anything.

We led him out to Riley's rented car. I kept my eyes on what was happening around me until we pulled away.

"Dad!" I reached forward from the back seat and squeezed his shoulder.

"Hey kiddo!" Dad smiled.

Michael Czrygy was a very handsome man with sandy blondish hair and eyes that made you feel like you were the only person on the planet. I'd seen him and Mom in DC when I'd been there, but that had been a rare visit. The truth was, I missed him.

"You promised to come over for dinner," I insisted.

"I wouldn't miss it for anything," Dad laughed. "By the way, I love what you've done with your hair."

I grimaced. "Yes, well, your girls are to blame for that." Dad had made quite an impression on my troop in DC, and they adored him.

"Will I get to see the troop?" he asked.

"I wasn't planning to bring them today."

Maybe I should've. My girls could take down any terrorist and show them how this was really done. They once took over Langley (CIA headquarters) and had men running in terror. The memory of that made me smile.

We arrived at the fertilizer plant in eleven minutes, due to a traffic jam of three cars at the only stoplight in town. Agent Savage spotted us right away and made his way toward us. He didn't look happy.

"Agent Andrews," he said with a stiff nod. "Ms. Wrath, what are you doing here?"

"They're with me, Savage." Dad appeared around the corner of the SUV. "Is there a problem?"

Agent Savage looked like he'd just swallowed something that came out of the south end of my cats. His face turned comically red, and he began to sputter. I wondered if his head would explode.

"Senator Czrygy! What are you doing here?"

"These are my constituents," Dad said, stepping forward. "And I'm here to show support for President Benson. Is there a problem? I can call Ed Jacobson…" Dad casually dropped Savage's boss's boss's boss's name as if he were going golfing with the man in ten minutes.

Savage considered this, "No. No problem, Senator." He turned and walked away stiffly.

"Well then," Dad said to us as he clapped his hands together. "Lead the way."

Riley headed for the factory, and I brought up the rear, behind my father. My head was swerving so much in an attempt to locate Red and Blue, I felt like my brain was swimming. This must be why the Secret Service were idiots—head bobbing must cause brain damage. Maybe I should be nicer to them.

Dad waved and greeted people as we went. He really was good. The man had represented Iowa for several terms now, and I was pretty sure he'd been to every town in the state. And his constituents loved him. His elections were always landslides against any opponent the other side could drum up. It was almost embarrassing.

People shouted their hellos as we passed, and to my surprise, Dad responded with that person's name almost every time. I say almost, because he didn't recognize one or two people which meant that they were probably from out of state.

I didn't like the idea of having my Dad in a dangerous situation, but he was our only way to get into the inner workings of this event. Savage had made it clear we weren't invited to his little party. As soon as we were out of the diminutive agent's line of vision, Riley and I split off from Dad. My father nodded at us and then began working the room.

"How do you think they're going to do it?" I asked Riley.

"The bomb?" He answered. "There's really only one place."

I agreed. "The boiler room. That's where I'd put it."

By placing explosives there, Red and Blue would build a huge blast that would most likely level the building and everyone in it. I led Riley across the floor of the factory to an exit door that said *Staff Only*.

Riley followed me through the door before pulling it closed behind him. We had to move quickly. If anyone had seen us, they'd come after us. And this was a party for two. A cement stairwell gave us the choice of up or down.

"Down here," I said as I started toward the stairs.

All the lights were on, but we moved carefully. Riley and I were armed, but there was no point drawing attention to ourselves if Red and Blue were still on the premises. We hit the ground floor and carefully opened a door that warned us to *Keep Out*.

The door creaked, which made me wince a little. We paused to see if anyone came running, but there was no response. Riley was right at my back. I could feel his breath on the back of my neck, and it made me tingle. Dammit. I did *not* need this right now.

I moved forward into the room. Like the stairwell, it was fully lit. Riley closed the door behind him without so much as a creak. Show-off.

"I don't see anyone," I whispered.

Riley disappeared to my right. I took the left, clearing every nook and cranny in the room. It felt like it took hours, and normally I'm not fond of being this close to explosives. But a bomb could be anywhere in this room. We had to make sure. Double sure. It was slow going, and every little sound made me jump, but eventually, Riley and I met in the middle.

"Nothing," Riley said. "I found nothing."

"Me neither. There's no bomb here."

"Let's go over it again, this time with you on the right," Riley said.

I worked even more slowly, looking for anything Riley might have missed. There were all the usual pipes, buttons, and lights, but nothing incendiary. I got down on my hands and knees and looked under everything with a gap beneath it. I stood on tiptoe to look on top of pipes. Nothing.

Once again, we met in the middle.

"It's clean," I said. "You find anything?"

Riley shook his head, "No. And it worries me."

"Because there's nothing here?"

"Because it must be somewhere else," Riley answered. "And we're running out of time."

I agreed. "We have to check the rest of the building. Which will be tough because there are people everywhere."

Dodging Savage was going to be tough. By now he's probably realized we weren't at the Senator's side. He might even be looking for us. We'd have to perform a sweep without getting caught. How I wished I still had some of my old spy tools. The ring with the small hypodermic that could knock out an elephant would have come in handy here.

I followed Riley back up the stairs, and we re-entered the main floor.

"I'll take the offices," Riley said. "You start at the other end of the building. We'll meet in the middle."

I nodded. "Call if you find anything."

Riley disappeared, and I turned to face the crowd. Damn. My watch said we had less than an hour before President Benson arrived. Visitors were all over the place, trying to get a good seat for the event. It was impossible to tell who was who. I tried to scan the audience, but if Red and Blue were in disguise, I'd miss them.

I kept my head down as I wove through the crowd. I didn't need Agent Savage coming after me. I listened as I went and heard snippets of conversation, but nothing that sounded menacing. Crowd control would be impossible at this point.

I reached the opposite end of the room in about ten minutes, which was disappointing. There wouldn't be any lightning quick action if something happened. If there was a bomb here, it would definitely create a massacre. Just what any terrorist agency would want.

So why were Red and Blue doing this? What was *their* motivation? Were they anti-government? That might be it because of the president's presence. Could they be from a foreign group? Evelyn was an assassin for the highest bidder, so that was a possibility. But then, the couple I overheard had pitch perfect Midwestern American accents. That wasn't easy for most nationalities to achieve. And if they did, my experience was that they slipped after a few minutes.

A foreign terrorist organization would make a huge name for themselves by killing the leader of the free world. It would put even the smallest group on the map in an historical way. Epic even. Maybe Red and Blue had turned on the U.S. and were someone's foot soldiers on the ground here.

Iowa was a perfect target. Hitting the wholesome, homegrown center of the nation—even without taking out President Benson—would drive fear into the American population. It would show that anyone can get to us anywhere in the U.S.—and that New York and other large cities weren't the only targets. Americans would be constantly paranoid if a place like Willow Grove blew up. They'd know that they aren't safe even in the smallest, most anonymous place in the country.

So what was Evelyn's angle? Why kill her? Was she supposed to place the bomb, but reneged? I'd love to think that she came to feel something for my troop and didn't want any part of hitting them where it hurt.

But then, Evelyn never really got to know the girls in DC. She never got to know any of us. Still, my mind kept settling on that as an answer. The terrorists had hired her to take out Willow Grove, and she'd refused. So they killed her.

I liked that answer. It would tie everything up neatly. But real life wasn't neat and tidy. There could be other explanations. Maybe Evelyn argued with them over money. They weren't going to pay her what they'd promised, and she bolted. Or maybe she just couldn't make it happen in their time frame. They could've gotten rid of her for that.

Ugh! I wasn't getting anywhere with this. And worst of all, I still had no idea why Evelyn had attached herself to my troop. How rude of her to go and die without answering these questions.

My mind kept going back to the puzzle box. She'd given it to Lauren just before she'd died. It had to be a message for me. Maybe Evelyn knew all along who I was. Maybe she was even hiding out in my troop, sizing me up. But why come to the church? Did she want to tell me something? Warn me? If so, why?

I shook my head. This wasn't getting solved right now, and I needed my brain for other things. The end of the building I was in was filled with machinery. I crawled around the best I could in a suit. My gun was crushed against the small of my back. It had been a long, long time since I'd worn a piece. Hopefully after this I'd never need to again.

None of the crowd had spilled over into this area, because the sight lines were bad. They wouldn't be able to see the president. I went over everything again, but found no blinking red lights…no counter rapidly approaching zero…and nothing ticking.

My cell rang, and I answered it.

"Wrath," Riley said. "Did you find anything?"

I shook my head in the deluded thought that he could see me. "Nothing. You?"

"I managed to check out the podium and underneath the bleachers. Nothing on this end."

We agreed to meet up on a catwalk that hung over the main area. Maybe the terrorists would strike from above, and we'd get lucky. At least we could see from up there. The problem was that we wouldn't be able to get to the floor quickly if we did see something.

Riley and I spoke to each other, but our eyes were scanning the crowd.

"They could be down there," Riley said. He banged his hand on the railing. "Dammit. They should've cancelled or rescheduled."

"Yes they should have," I agreed. "But they didn't. And my father is down there. So I'll do whatever it takes to stop whatever is going to happen."

"I feel like an idiot," Riley said glumly. "This whole thing is idiotic. We have absolutely no way of knowing how or when they'll strike. We don't even know who they are."

"We've been in some bad situations before," I said. "But never one with so little intel."

I thought about Rex. I hadn't gotten a chance to talk to him before we left. I should have. I should've made a plan for the cats if I did get blown up. And I should've set up an educational trust fund for Finn. And I should've somehow said goodbye to the girls in my troop. Why hadn't I done any of that? If I survived this thing, those would be my first priorities. Well, not saying goodbye to the girls, because if I survived this, I was going to make damn sure this wouldn't happen again.

The thought of never seeing Rex again got to me. My stomach sank as I pictured him at my funeral, throwing himself over the coffin, weeping that I was his whole reason for living. That would be nice. But then, I saw Dr. Soo Jin Body comforting him. And then they'd fall for each other and get married. My cats would become her cats. They'd have gorgeous kids, and everyone would forget I existed.

"Wrath…" Riley said.

Well that wasn't going to happen! How could he marry her after I got myself blown up to save America?

"Wrath!" Riley said. "What is it? Your knuckles are completely white from gripping the railing so hard."

What? Oh. Right. I relaxed and let go of the railing, rubbing my hands together.

"What is it? Do you see something?" Riley persisted.

"No," I said slowly. "I'm just furious that something could happen here, and we can't do anything about it."

Something was happening down on the floor. A bunch of men in suits came down the aisle toward the podium. I could see President Benson's graying head in the middle of the group. I looked to the stage to see Dad sitting there. It was time.

My heart started hammering beneath my ribs. At any minute, we would be blown to bits. I tore my focus away from home and onto the floor of the factory. People were clapping and waving at the president. Everyone seemed happy.

Well, everyone except for Agent Savage. He stood directly in front of the stage, facing the crowd. Just for a moment, I kind of hoped they'd swarm the stage like it was a rave. Did he really think that he alone could take on this crowd?

The clock was ticking…probably on a big bomb somewhere, and I couldn't do anything. I thought back to times in the field, when I'd been an agent. Had there ever been a time where I felt so exposed? A time when I felt so hopeless? Nope. Not one. Mainly because we had better intelligence, and we weren't related to the people who were in danger.

Dad spotted me from the stage and nodded. If he was worried, Senator Czrygy didn't show it. He was so awesome like that. Maybe he thought we had it all in hand. That was a depressing thought. Dad thought the threat was neutralized when in fact, there wasn't anything we could do. I felt guilty. I should've said goodbye to him too.

The president brought his hands up and motioned for everyone to sit down. He should've used the Girl Scout quiet sign. Although that would really only work if he was addressing a roomful of little girls. But if that had been the case, I knew Agent Savage would've been screwed.

"Anything?" Riley's voice was calm, but I sensed a slight undercurrent of panic.

"No," My voice cracked. "What do we do?"

He didn't answer me. Instead, Riley focused on the floor below. Well, I guess if we were going to die, we could at least really witness it well.

"This is insane," I said. "It's completely out of our control."

Riley nodded but didn't look at me. I didn't like it that he agreed. I wanted him to say something like, *aha—there's the bad guys—I can see the bomb and disarm it from here…*

But he didn't.

"What did we miss?" Riley said through a tight jaw.

I shrugged. "Everything. Nothing. I don't know. But we didn't find anything. The Secret Service didn't find anything. Everyone coming through the doors was wanded, so no one could've brought the bomb in or worn it."

President Benson was droning on about agricultural things. I think I might have heard something on ethanol and chickens, but I wasn't sure. He should talk about pigs. We have a lot of pigs in Iowa.

"I'm going crazy up here," I said. "I'm going down to the floor."

Riley looked at me. "To do what?"

"I don't know. But whatever it is, I can do it better down there."

Riley stayed up on the catwalk, and I carefully made my way down the metal stairs, trying to tread silently. The echo factor was ridiculous here. I hit the floor and glanced back up at Riley. He didn't look at me.

Okay, Genius, what now? Coming downstairs seemed like a good idea at the time. But now I had to actually do something. So I took up a position against the side wall, scanning the audience in profile. I gave up after a few moments because it's really hard to find two bad guys in a crowd of a couple hundred people.

I started to pace back and forth in the back of the room, behind the audience. Every now and then I caught Savage's eye and he glowered. I ignored him. My presence was a reminder that I didn't think he could handle his job. I hoped I was right. Nothing would make me feel better than to be proved wrong.

The minutes ticked by in my head like the bomb I thought was somewhere in this building. We were running out of time. My life was ticking away. In a moment of desperation, I grabbed two state troopers hanging out in the back of the room and sent one to the boiler room and one to the offices.

That felt a little better. The Iowa State Police are extremely competent. They didn't even question me. They just went and did what I'd asked them too. If only other agencies were like this.

I stepped up behind the bleachers and very carefully searched beneath the audience. It was dark from so many legs and backs. I turned on the flashlight app on my cell, but kept it dim as I swept back and forth. Nothing.

By the time I emerged from beneath the bleachers, the troopers reappeared. They informed me that they'd found nothing and took up positions against the back wall.

I texted Riley, *What are we missing here?*

President Benson is wrapping up was all he texted back.

My eyes swept the room—well, what I could see at least. Every word the president spoke ticked like the second hand on a huge, judgey clock. It felt a little like I was moving through water, unable to maintain a pace.

Applause erupted, startling me, and I jumped backward, landing in a defensive position. If the troopers saw me, they said nothing. I liked them even more. Blood pulsed in my ears. This was it. If there was going to be an explosion, it would be now. I closed my eyes tightly—as if that would protect me.

In my mind, I saw the photo we'd found. Blue and Red, looking at a map of Iowa, with the letters G 11. G 11 on the map meant Willow Grove. I'd proved that on my atlas. Wait…my mind reached out to the photo again. The map! It wasn't part of a spiral bound atlas. It was a single, folding map. Like the ones you find in rest areas throughout the state.

I raced up to one of the troopers as the crowd started toward the exits.

"Do you have a state map in your car?" I asked.

The trooper nodded. I asked him to go get it, and he disappeared. I really liked these guys. They were the perfect professionals.

"Here you go." The trooper returned, handing me the map.

The crowd was encompassing us now, and I pushed through until I came to the staircase where Riley was waiting. I opened the map and held it out in front of me. Damn. It was too detailed to do by eye.

"What is it?" Riley asked as I got down on my knees and spread the map on the floor.

"I think we made a mistake," I said as I found G with my left hand and 11 with my right. Very slowly, I began to bring my hands together.

"My atlas is at least ten years old," I explained as my fingers got closer to each other.

"Who has a ten-year-old atlas?" Riley scoffed.

"Someone who bought it at a garage sale, and someone who didn't think she'd ever need one," I answered. My fingers came together, and my heart stopped. I started over and did it again in case I was wrong.

"Why should that matter?" Riley got down on his knees next to me.

"Because I remember something in the paper when I'd first moved here. Something about the atlas being recalled."

Riley's right eyebrow went up. "I've never heard of an atlas being recalled."

"Well it was." My fingers came together and I gasped. "Because there had been mistakes." I looked at Riley. "G 11 isn't for Willow Grove. G 11 is for Who's There. They're going to blow up my hometown."

CHAPTER NINETEEN

———

"Hey kiddo," Dad said quietly, and I looked at his shoes. "What's up?"

Riley and I scrambled to our feet. "We've got to go, Senator," Riley said as he took my father's arm.

"Well, well, well." Agent Savage appeared in front of us with a sneer on his face. "I guess someone owes me an apology."

The man looked like he'd won the lottery on his birthday while drinking from the fountain of youth. He was going to enjoy this. In his little amoeba brain, I'd fall all over myself apologizing in front of the Senator who oversaw his agency.

"Sorry," I said as I took Dad's other arm and we started hurrying him away.

"Sorry?" Savage roared. He ran up and cut us off. "Sorry? You question my ability to do my job, somehow trick the Senator into bringing you here, get us all worked up over nothing, and all you have to say is 'sorry'?"

I shoved him aside and shouted over my shoulder as I rushed past him, "Yup."

We kept moving, but once again, Savage blocked us.

"No!" He shouted. "You owe me one hell of an apology! The CIA owes me one hell of an apology! And the Senator should investigate your Agency because of your profound incompetence!"

Savage's face was an alarming shade of red. Riley got all up in his grille (I learned that phrase from my troop), and the two men began a testosterone-ish pheromonal exchange without words.

I stepped up between them. "Like I said, sorry. You did your job. Yay. Good for you."

"Hey!" Savage said as Riley and I started to lead Dad away. "Senator! Are you going to say something?"

We kept moving. Savage yanked on my arm. "Honey— you're going to be out of a job!"

Honey?

He continued, "I'm going to make sure the Senator truly understands what's happening here, and when I'm done, you won't even be allowed to apply for a school crossing guard job."

"Good luck," I said as I brought my fist down on his forearm hitting the sweet spot—a little trick I knew. His grip released instantly, and rather involuntarily too. "Because, Honey, Senator Czrygy is my father."

We left a huffing secret service agent in our wake as we continued to Riley's SUV.

"I thought you didn't want anyone to know about our connection," Dad said with amusement as he buckled his seat belt.

"Yeah, well, incognito is overrated," I responded as Riley fired up the engine and we raced, hell bent for leather, for Who's There and our possible destruction…for the second time today.

I filled Dad in on the way, and he finally looked concerned.

Rex was waiting for us at the door of the station when we arrived. He led us to a conference room and sent Kevin to fetch us some coffee as I smoothed out the map on the table and told him what I thought was really happening.

He didn't look happy.

"You think this town was the original target," he said finally.

I nodded. "I got so carried away with the fact that the president was going to be here, I didn't double-check. I should've double-checked. It was just stupidity that I didn't."

Riley opened his mouth. It looked like he was about to give me crap about the recalled atlas, but then he changed his mind.

"Don't feel too bad. With the president next-door, I would've thought the same," Rex said. "There's no real big target here. No major events, nothing."

"I know. It sounds insane," I agreed. "But G 11 points to Who's There. Evelyn showed up in Who's There and inconveniently dropped dead here. And Red and Blue didn't leave town when they should have. They took up residence in the old Philips' place."

"That old house outside of town?" Dad asked. "I always liked that place."

"Which made me think, why stick around if they were really just here to get Evelyn? There isn't any reason to do this. They would've been free and clear to leave," I said, pausing to accept a cup of coffee from Kevin. I drank it before remembering that I don't drink coffee. I took another gulp.

"And then there was Seamus Bailey. Why come back and kill him? They could've hit the road, never to be seen again. It was unlikely Seamus could describe them with any accuracy. Why come back to silence him?"

Rex nodded. "Because they weren't leaving."

"Because," Riley added. "They were afraid of him seeing them again. Because they were sticking around."

"Exactly."

We stood there, staring at each other.

"This is the target, for some reason," I repeated. "And our two terrorists are still out there."

"They're not at the Philips' place," Rex frowned. "I've had it under surveillance since that night."

"So where are they?" Dad asked as Kevin handed him a donut. Where did Kevin get donuts? Is Kevin capable of sharing?

I shook my head. "I don't know. They could be anywhere."

"Well at least Evelyn's body is back in the morgue," Rex said. "Ted has beefed up security, so they'd have a fight on their hands if they show up."

Riley stared off into space. "I still don't understand why they wanted her body. It's not like she'd have the puzzle box on her."

"Puzzle box?" Dad asked as he wiped the powdered sugar from the donut off his chin. It's a good thing Mom wasn't here. She never let him eat crap like this.

Riley filled Dad in on Evelyn giving Lauren the puzzle box and how we found the photo there.

"So Evelyn had proof, and they wanted to silence her?" Dad asked.

"Yes," Rex said. "But they'd have to know the body would've been stripped."

I shook my head. "It's a photo. She could've hidden it anywhere."

"Like inside of her?" Kevin squeaked.

We all turned to face him. It was like a plant or two-by-four talking for the first time.

"Cuz that would be gross!" Kevin added.

"Officer Dooley," Rex said with the patience of Job. "Please go and get us some bottles of water."

Kevin fled. Maybe speaking out loud even freaked him out. I hadn't heard him say anything even remotely helpful since the sixth grade.

"The coroner would've found the photo if it had been anywhere on or in the body," Rex said.

"So, why did they need the corpse?" Riley asked. "We already knew who she was. We didn't need her remains for that."

"There's a reason we aren't thinking of," I said. "Which could mean they'll be back for it."

The room cleared out before Kevin could return. As we drove to the hospital, me with Rex and Dad with Riley, I pictured him walking in with water bottles, seeing us gone, and hanging his head.

"You think there are explosives in the body?" Rex said as we raced across town.

"It's a possibility. The autopsy was done. There'd be no need to examine it again."

"That's pretty horrible." Rex's jaw was tight.

"Terrorists do it in the Persian Gulf," I said.

"Wouldn't Soo Jin notice any new scars?" Rex asked.

I shrugged. "Not if they used the ones she made during the autopsy."

"How much can you insert into a human body?"

I shook my head. "It depends on what types of explosives are used. This isn't my area of expertise at all. Too bad we don't have a bomb squad in town."

"So what's the next step?" Rex asked. "Do we cut her open in an attempt to disarm her—or do we just take her out into the middle of a cornfield and set her off?"

"I don't know." My mind was reeling. I wondered if Evelyn had ever thought it would come to this.

"So, who are they?" Rex asked. "Who's the couple, and what do they want?"

I didn't want to say *I don't know* again. It was a crappy option for someone in my field. But I didn't have a clue. Whoever Red and Blue really were didn't matter as much as disarming the bomb.

Rex didn't wait for me to answer. "So the hospital was the target?"

I shrugged again. "It just might be."

"Why the hospital? Why not the fertilizer plant where they'd kill more people?"

"It's most likely a sleeper cell. They don't like to change plans. And they usually end contact with their handlers once the orders are given. My best guess—the thing with the president was a very recent addition. Red and Blue decided to stick with the original plan."

"They must be very stupid," Rex said. "Thank God for that."

I nodded as we pulled up to the hospital. "Terrorists, domestic or foreign, usually have a very narrow view of things. They think they are soldiers to their cause and are one hundred percent focused on the job. They have blinders on that block out any peripheral vision. All they know is that they are doing this for a reason, and that they have to succeed. Intelligence is nice but not mandatory."

Rex parked alongside Riley and we all piled out and started running for the door. Ted Dooley met us, and we all headed to the morgue.

"I evacuated as many as I could," Ted said. "I sent for ambulances from Des Moines, but they won't be here for twenty minutes."

He looked worried. His white hair was plastered to his head, and he was sweating. Poor guy. He probably thought nothing like this would ever happen here. I still couldn't figure out how this guy was Kevin's father. Maybe the good genes skip a generation in that family.

Dr. Body was waiting and led us into a cold room with Evelyn's body on a table. The doctor had covered up what she could out of modesty, but her abdomen was on full display, with a zipper-like scar right down the middle.

"These stitches—" she pointed to a section in the center, about ten inches long "—are new. They aren't mine. My guess is that's where the explosives would be."

I studied Soo Jin. She was calm and collected. If she was terrified about blowing up, she didn't show it. I liked that. Maybe she wasn't so bad after all. Maybe she'd be a good owner of Moneypenny and Bond. I cringed a little—thinking of losing those two kitties still bothered me.

Riley stepped forward. "Clear out. I'll do it." He picked up a scalpel and waited for us to leave.

We didn't.

"You don't have a lot of experience in defusing bombs, Riley," I said evenly.

He looked at me. "And you do? I've defused two bombs, which I'd guess is two more than anyone else in here."

I looked around. Nobody argued with him.

"I'm not leaving," I said, folding my arms over my chest. "We're in this together. Might as well blow ourselves up together."

Rex's cell rang, and we all jumped. He took the call out to the hallway.

"You," Riley pointed the scalpel at me, "and everyone else are leaving. I'm not making one cut until you go."

Rex burst through the door. "Des Moines can't send anyone to help. They've got their own problems."

"What do you mean?" I asked.

"Red and Blue were found at the airport."

"So they have them?" Dad asked.

Rex shook his head. "Not really. They've taken hostages and shut down the airport."

"Can't SWAT take them out?" Ted asked. "I might be wrong, but can't they just shoot them?"

"No. They're both wearing suicide vests. One shot and Des Moines will need to build a new airport."

"We're on our own," I said. Dammit.

CHAPTER TWENTY

———

"In light of that intel, I'd say the odds of a bomb in this body are about one hundred percent," Riley said. "Which means you all have to go."

I disagreed. I'm stubborn like that. "I'm staying. Everyone else should go though."

Dad wore a grim face. "If Merry stays, I stay."

I turned to him. "Dad—I'm not a baby, and this isn't the first time I've been in danger. You need to go. Mom doesn't need to lose both of us."

Rex said, "Senator, you need to go." He nodded to Ted. "Please take him out to the car in the parking lot."

Ted agreed. "I'll take him out, but I'm coming back in. I'll do all I can to get the other patients to safety."

"Merry," Dad protested.

I put up a hand to stop him. "Go!"

My father sighed, then followed the director of security out the door.

I turned to Dr. Body, "You should go too, Soo Jin."

"I think I should stay," she said a little hesitantly. "You need an expert here. What if the explosives are hidden beneath organs or muscle tissue?"

"I don't think we need to handle Evelyn with kid gloves anymore, do you?" Riley said. "If I have to tear her apart, I'll do so. Wrath is right. You need to go."

The medical examiner started to protest, but Rex cut her off. "You should go help evacuate the rest of the patients. They'll need all the doctors they can get."

Dr. Body looked carefully at each and every one of us, her eyes finally settling on Rex. Oh for crying out loud! Was she going to flirt with him right in front of me? If I didn't explode in the next few minutes, I might rethink giving her the kittens.

She finally gave a little nod and fled the room a little too quickly. I guess she wasn't as calm as I thought. As for me, my heart was beating a merengue that was giving me a migraine. I looked at Rex.

He shook his head. "I'm not leaving, Merry."

I started to protest. I was going to say something about him staying alive long enough to take care of my cats, but to be perfectly honest—I was glad he was here. Then when I vomited from watching Riley desecrate the corpse, he could step up and help Riley.

"Fine," Riley said.

He pulled an overhead light closer to Evelyn and placed the scalpel on the sutures. After a moment's hesitation, he started cutting through the black threads. Rex and I stepped closer. It was so quiet we could hear the blade cutting through the thread. I was pretty sure we were all holding our breath too.

I'd decided that it was in our best interest not to talk at all. First of all, because I didn't want to distract Riley, and secondly, because I've never disarmed anything more difficult than cutting the fuse on dynamite. And even if I did know a thing or two, I was rusty.

I was staying for support. At least, I'd like to think my presence was helping. And for some very weird reason, I was staying for Evelyn. Somebody should be on her side, right? Even though she was a traitor and bad guy—she had gone on the trip with us, and she tried to warn us by giving Lauren the puzzle box. Which is all pretty weird because she could've just stopped by my house.

Of course, it didn't undo all the horrible things she'd done—even though I didn't know exactly what they were. But it was something, and the woman deserved to have someone by her side as Riley sliced through her remains.

Riley was locked in concentration. He had a focus I could only admire. I tended to get distracted easily these days.

Riley had this gift of tuning out the whole world to focus on one thing. And if anything deserved his full attention, it was this.

He wasn't taking any chances. Riley cut about four inches longer on each side of the new stitches. No point in having to backtrack if needed. After the last snip, he put on latex gloves and gently eased the body open.

I wasn't too squeamish. When I'd said I'd probably vomit earlier, it was from the tension. Not seeing the body. I could feel my blood pressure spike as Rex stepped even closer and brought the light down closer to the body. I didn't move.

Riley whistled. That wasn't good. I didn't ask. Like I said, I didn't want to break his concentration. But I did notice that vein in Rex's neck throbbing. This seemed bad. Really bad. Neither man spoke. Riley just bent closer to the cavity and moved his fingers around.

There's no way around it. Bombs are scary. And now that they could be controlled by cell phone, they were even scarier. But with Blue and Red holding off a whole SWAT team in Des Moines, I doubted they were even thinking of the Evelyn Bomb. Still, it was just one more factor in the stress fog that seemed to fill the room.

My thoughts drifted back to Evelyn again. By now, I was pretty sure she'd tagged along with my troop on the DC trip to hide out. It was a good cover, but she was taking the chance that someone would ID her. But why did she pick me? And why did she implicate me in that fax?

It was possible the fax was sent by Red and Blue to cover their tracks. I guess we'd never really know what Evelyn had been thinking. All we knew was that she'd turned down this job and tried to warn us. That redeemed her a little in my eyes. I really didn't want to know what she'd done to betray her country. It didn't seem to matter now.

We were no closer to figuring out who Red and Blue were. But if the Des Moines police managed to capture them alive, we'd find out. It wasn't as important as defusing this bomb and saving my town.

Rex's phone started buzzing on his hip, but he ignored it. This was more important. This had precedence. There was some commotion in the hall. Probably something with the evacuation.

Dooley could handle it. Ted Dooley that is. Kevin Dooley couldn't handle his own breathing without opening his mouth.

After a few agonizing minutes, Riley stood up straight and put down the scalpel. A light sheen of perspiration had broken out across his forehead. That wasn't good. Rex turned to me and shook his head.

"You can't do it..." I murmured.

Riley shook his head. "I can't do it."

"There's a bomb, then?" I asked even though it was a statement of fact now.

"C-4. Lots of it. In plastic bags to keep it dry. And I don't understand the trigger mechanism. It's something I've never seen before."

Great.

"Is there a timer?" That would've been convenient so we knew how much time we had left.

"We have five minutes to figure out what to do next," Rex said.

Oh. So there really was a timer. At least we knew how long it would be before we turned into a red mist.

"So how do we dispose of the body in that short amount of time?" I asked as I ran over to a rolling cot and started dragging it over.

Riley shook his head and took off his gloves. "I'm afraid to even move it. That could set it off. And there are lots of wires. I have no idea which one to cut."

"Isn't it always the red one?" I asked. It was always the red one in movies.

"So, we run," Riley said as he ripped off the rubber gloves.

"Let's go..." I said.

The commotion in the hallway was getting closer and louder. Maybe the three of us could help somehow. The morgue was in the basement. It could bring down this entire wing. Hopefully we could save a few lives...

The noise got louder. It sounded familiar. I saw movement outside the opaque door window.

Oh no...

Kelly burst through the door with the four Kaitlins, the two Hannahs, Lauren, and Betty. The girls were laughing.

"Let's all thank Dr. Body for this spooky, late night morgue tour!" Kelly said brightly as she led the girls into the room.

She stopped short when she saw us gaping at her. Then she saw the body.

"What's going on?" she said as she raced to cover up the body.

Then she saw the open cavity and looked inside. I can only imagine she saw the bomb inside. What were they doing here? How the hell had this happened? A late night morgue tour? Why wouldn't I know about that?

I turned to the door just in time to hear a lock clicking. I tried the handle, but we weren't going anywhere.

"What the—" I looked at the girls and decided not to swear, "—are you doing here? We didn't have anything scheduled!"

"Is that a dead body?" Betty cried out.

"Cool!" Lauren and one of the Hannahs said in unison as they stepped closer.

"Dr. Body called…she told us it was a slow night and would be a great time for a visit…" Kelly's normally calm demeanor was cracking.

One of the Kaitlins ran over and threw her arms around my waist. "We're having a haunted lock-in!"

Rex was beating a fire extinguisher against the three-by-three-foot glass in the door. It wasn't breaking, but he kept at it with a fury I'd never seen before.

The girls started to advance on the body, and Kaitlin joined them, but Kelly dove in front of the table, refusing to let them go any further. I looked around for a spot to store the girls when the bomb went off.

"This is bad, isn't it?" Kelly asked.

I ran to the walk-in freezer and tugged on the door handle. It wouldn't open. How could something like this be locked from the inside? I shot a glance to Riley. He set his jaw and picked up the scalpel. He turned to the body and started poking around.

We were trapped. Locked in with a bomb. Dr. Body had betrayed us. She'd set this whole thing up. I should've seen it coming. She was new to town. She was the only witness to Red and Blue stealing the body. And now she'd called my girls and Kelly here and locked us in.

That was the big one. Taking out children would be a coup for anyone trying to hit America where it hurt. The patients in the hospital were just frosting on the ticking cake.

Kelly and I stared at each other for a second. Then I grabbed the cart and knocked it on its side. I ordered the girls to sit down behind it. They seemed confused but the gleam of terror in their leaders' eyes must've made them compliant because they did what I asked quickly and quietly.

Riley was in a full sweat now, and Rex had his gun in his hand, trying to decide if he could shoot through the glass. The space would be just big enough to toss the kids through, hopefully before the bomb went off. But it was possible that shooting the door would fail and even cause a ricochet. It was a tough decision.

Kelly was dragging another metal table over in an attempt to make a protective shell for the girls. It was a long shot, but what else could we do? I joined her, putting that table over the girls' heads.

Rex started kicking the door at what was usually its weakest point—right at the latch. He wasn't having much luck, but he kept trying. Riley was engrossed in trying one more time to deactivate the bomb.

As soon as we had our little metal igloo built, I shoved Kelly in there with the girls. She didn't resist. She had a baby at home who needed her. My goddaughter, Finn. There was no way she wasn't going home in one piece tonight if I could help it.

The girls were remarkably calm. I've never been more proud of them. Hopefully we'd live through this, and I could tell them that.

I joined Riley. Rex was still banging at the door. I couldn't help him. Not that I could help Riley either, but maybe a miracle would happen, and I'd know what to do. That would be nice.

"What's the status?" I asked, looking down into Evelyn.

"Two minutes left, and I think I've narrowed it down to these three wires." He showed me three red wires. Why did they all have to be red?

"You're guessing?" I asked.

Riley turned his eyes to me. "What do you want me to do? I have a thirty-three percent chance of getting it right."

Rex stopped banging at the door. Out of breath and sweating, he came to the other side of the table. Maybe he thought he could help too.

"If we don't die here," I said quietly so the girls wouldn't hear, "I'm going to take Soo Jin apart, piece by piece."

"Not helping," Riley said, his full attention back on the wires. His scalpel moved back and forth, hovering for a few seconds over each wire.

"One minute," Rex said.

He looked at me and gave a weak smile. I nodded and smiled back. So this was how it was going to end. Blown up by a corpse bomb in a morgue in Who's There, Iowa. I always thought I'd die in Uzbekistan or Kazakhstan or one of the -stans. Or maybe Iceland. You never really knew in my former line of work.

Rex looked down at the bomb. "Thirty seconds."

This is not the way we are going out! I wasn't going to let that happen. I closed my eyes in an attempt at achieving bomb disposal nirvana.

"Twenty..." Rex droned on.

No! There had to be something I could do. But what?

"Ten..."

Think Wrath, think!

"Nine..."

Riley looked up at me. "I'm so sorry. There are things I never said to you and now won't get the chance."

If Rex didn't like Riley's statement, he didn't acknowledge it. He really was a great guy.

"Eight..."

"It's okay," I replied. "Really." I didn't want to hear what Riley would say. I wasn't emotionally prepared for anything.

"Seven..."

"Merry...Finn..." Riley ignored my plea. "You have always been..."

"Six..."

My eyes grew wide. A desperate idea formed around the edges of my mind.

"Five..."

"...very important to me..." Riley continued.

"Four..."

I held up my hand to stop Riley. I didn't want to have any weirdness, and I needed to think.

"Three..."

"Cut all three cords!" I screamed.

Riley looked startled.

"Two..."

"Do it! Do it now!" I shouted.

"One..."

Riley stuck the scalpel under the three wires and brought it up hard, severing the three wires.

I closed my eyes and waited.

Nothing happened.

"It stopped!" Rex said.

Screw worrying about ricochets. I took my gun and fired at the window. It took four shots to shatter. Rex ran over, reached outside, and unlocked the door.

"Come on!" I said as I started tearing the metal tables off of Kelly and the girls.

They were out the door in seconds with Kelly barking orders. She knew this place better than I did. They'd be safe very soon.

I slumped against a wall. I was completely spent. Stupid adrenaline.

"How did you know?" Riley asked, a stunned look on his face.

"What?" I asked. My brain was all messed up.

"How did you know to cut the three wires?" Riley asked again.

I shook my head. "I didn't. I just guessed. And hey, it worked!"

Now I just needed to find that evil coroner and show her a new way to use a scalpel…

CHAPTER TWENTY-ONE

———

Riley turned to extricate the bomb from Evelyn as Rex walked up and pulled me against him. Before I could speak his lips were on mine. I'd heard that living through dangerous situations made people…um…amorous, but I'd never experienced it before. Usually in the field after something huge happened, I just took a nap.

This kiss was something I'd never experienced before. It was primal, animal, and I loved it. After a few seconds, I pulled away in an attempt to catch my breath. Rex smiled before letting me go.

If Riley saw the kiss, he didn't say so. He was just lifting the bomb out of Evelyn's abdomen when we'd stopped. Rex gave me a wink and drew his gun.

"We'd better go get Dr. Body," he said.

I looked to Riley as I drew my own gun.

"Go. Now. Don't let her get away," my former handler said.

I ran ahead of Rex, but he was close on my heels. It was weird running through a hospital. Every fiber of my being screamed, *don't run in the hospital.* It was like my brain was trying to trip up my feet.

"I think we should head outside. She wouldn't be in here if she thought it was going to blow," Rex said. But I wasn't listening. I'd heard a noise that sounded like yelling.

"You go," I ordered. I didn't tell him why. He would've just argued with me. "I want to check something out."

Rex nodded but looked a little uneasy.

"I'll be fine. Go!"

I watched as he ran off toward the exit. I'd definitely heard someone. It was probably nothing, but what if one of my girls decided to take a detour to outside? I'd better check to make sure.

Good thing the hospital only had two floors. I was starting to get a little lightheaded. I didn't run much. Maybe I should take it up when this was over. I've heard of jogging with your dog…but could you jog with cats?

The building was empty—at least this floor was. There was no one to stop me at any of the desks, and room after room was empty. Maybe I imagined it.

Dr. Body was probably watching for an explosion from somewhere in town. That had to be a shock when nothing happened. I smiled as I passed through the east wing. It made me happy to think she was somewhere, cursing the bomb for not working. Or maybe cursing because I wasn't dead.

Who was she? Where had she come from, and who in Human Resources was stupid enough to hire a terrorist? I stopped and gasped for breath, doubled over and panting. As a terrorist, she was Korean. But South Korea wouldn't have sent a spy to blow up small town Iowa. And the North Koreans barely had the resources to support the very idea of a mission, let alone actually attempting it.

She'd said she came from San Francisco. Not exactly a seething hotbed of terrorist activity. But maybe she lied. To be perfectly honest, I was a little thrilled that she was the bad guy. Now I wouldn't have to worry about her flirting with Rex and Riley. And I wouldn't even rub their noses in it. Not even once.

And the best part? This psycho wasn't getting my kittens. It really was a win-win. Now I just had to finish searching the hospital before going wide and taking the town apart bit by bit until I found her.

I gave up on running and walked quickly through the remaining corridors. This was a bust. No one was in here. I'd probably heard a radio or someone very loud outside. Besides, Rex might need help finding this Soo Jin. I wondered how Riley and Rex had missed seeing who and what she really was.

In fact, I was a little upset with myself that I hadn't seen through her either. I guess I was too distracted with Riley moving in and Soo Jin's charms. It didn't matter. Once I found her, I was going to kill her. She'd dragged Kelly and my Scouts into this mess. She'd killed Evelyn at our sleepover and marched them into certain danger with the bomb. Oh yeah. She was going down. I knew Rex and Riley would need her alive, but maybe it'd be alright if she was missing a few pieces.

I came around the corner near the lobby and spotted some movement in the security office. Ted must still be here— he must've come back in once Rex told him the bomb had been defused. I should fill him in. I walked up to the opaque, glass door and turned the knob.

"You're not going to get away with this!" a woman shouted.

Uh-oh. Soo Jin must've realized the bomb didn't go off, so she came in and took Dooley's secretary as a hostage. Wouldn't she be surprised when I marched in and shot her? I pressed against the door, and walked in.

I wasn't prepared for what I saw.

"You?" I asked. "You did this?"

The head of security was holding Dr. Body in front of him, a gun leveled at her head. It wasn't the secretary I'd heard. It was Soo Jin. She looked terrified.

"How did you defuse that bomb?" Ted snarled.

"If you thought it would blow up, why did you stay here?" I asked, raising my gun to aim at his head.

"I wasn't!" Dooley snapped. "I was in the parking lot in my van. But when the hospital didn't go boom, I knew something was wrong."

"And you came back inside to find out," I finished.

He nodded and pressed the gun more firmly against Dr. Body's temple.

"You called Kelly and told her to come here," I said.

He shook his head, "No, that was my secretary, Mavis."

Just then, Mavis appeared behind me, and I felt a gun in my lower back. I glanced back to make sure it really was her.

"Why?" I asked, without lowering my gun. I wasn't giving up without a fight.

Ted Dooley's eyes narrowed, "Money, of course. I was getting paid eight figures just to blow up a hospital." He nodded at the woman, who was still behind me, still holding a gun on me. "We're going to the Caribbean as soon as we take care of you two."

"What's your connection to Red and Blue?" I stalled. Okay, it wasn't so much of a stall as curiosity. I hadn't seen this coming. And it kind of pissed me off.

"My handlers," Ted said. He was relaxed, confident he could pull this off. "They're from a paramilitary group in Idaho."

Ugh. Idiot militants. I hated idiot militants. "And Evelyn? What's the deal with her?"

He shrugged. "I'm afraid you're going to have to die with that one unanswered. All I know is that she was hiding out from them because they wanted her to do this job. She balked. They hired me instead."

That seemed too easy after all the thought I'd put into figuring this out. Could it really be that simple? I thought about it. Okay, I could see Evelyn coming here to scout out the job. She changed her mind and went on the run, hiding with my troop in the one place these anti-government militia members wouldn't ever go—the nation's capital.

But that was only a theory. Evelyn was dead and unable to tell us what really happened. I'd have to grill Red and Blue for that. And where in hell was Rex? Or even Riley? Even if they'd finished what they were doing, wouldn't they come looking for me? I had to keep stalling.

"Why would you blow up your own town?" I asked. "And what about your son, Kevin?" Personally, I loathed Kevin, but it was strange that the officer's dad was the terrorist.

"Don't remind me," Ted rolled his eyes. "That kid is a moron."

"He's your son!" I argued. Sure, I agreed with the man. But it still seemed pretty cold for his father to talk about him like that.

"Barely," Dooley complained. "That boy has been a mouth-breather from day one. We haven't seen each other in years."

That seemed a bit harsh and somewhat impossible. How do you live in a town this size and not run into your own kid? I now felt sorry for Kevin.

"So it's all about the money?"

Dooley laughed, "Of course! You don't think it's political, do you? Well, it was with Red and Blue, but not me. I'd blow up my own mother for eight figures."

Something inside me snapped. You do not disrespect your mother. I launched my head back as hard as I could, connecting with the skull of the woman behind me. She dropped her gun, and I grabbed her, pulling her in front of me, with my gun to her head. Now we each had a hostage. Now things were even. I had no idea where I was going with this, but at least the odds were better. If I could just hold out until Rex or Riley showed up...

"Let her go!" Ted growled. There was a timbre in his voice that told me he was really angry.

Good.

"Not until you let Dr. Body go," I insisted.

We stood there, facing each other, each holding a woman at gunpoint, over a no man's land of nice, shag carpeting.

"I don't trust you," he sneered.

"I don't trust you either. So we're at a standstill until help arrives." Where were those guys?

To her credit, Mavis didn't whine or whimper. She was tough as nails and probably thought her lover would come through for her. She shouldn't have thought that. He wasn't leaving here unless it was in handcuffs, with a few "accidental" bullet holes.

Dooley was thinking hard. Apparently, he didn't have a plan in case of his girlfriend being held at gunpoint. I ran the risk of him shooting her, just to escape. He betrayed his own son, so why not his girlfriend?

And if that happened, the bullet could hit me. But I'd certainly gun him down. Hopefully missing Soo Jin in the process. I felt a little bad about suspecting her. But how could I know? Kelly had said Dr. Body called her. Since Kelly had only briefly met her, she wouldn't recognize her voice. And Mavis must have disguised hers.

Something moved out of the corner of my eye. A dark shape flashed by the office door. About damn time! I didn't care if it was Rex or Riley or Evelyn's reanimated corpse. Someone was out there listening.

"I'll give you a few more seconds to decide," I said.

Ted Dooley's arm was starting to shake. Apparently I wasn't the only one out of shape. I tried to remember the layout of the offices. Was there another way in here? There should be a fire exit. We were on the ground floor, but still. I pictured the cavalry riding to the rescue. If things went well, they'd come up behind Dooley. But I'd take any help I could get.

"You won't shoot her," Dooley finally said. "People like you don't kill."

"Well you seem to have no problem with that," I snapped. "You were more than willing to invite my whole troop and co-leader to your bomb bay."

He shrugged, "Collateral damage. I would've killed Red and Blue too, if they weren't only going to pay me once I got out of town."

A thought occurred to me. "And what makes you think they would actually do that? Militias don't have that kind of money. You're a pawn. You've been used. Give it up before someone gets shot."

The blood drained out of his face, and I felt Mavis gasp. Huh. They hadn't thought of that. It's pretty stupid to take an assignment like this without doing some checking first. He was only doing this for the money. If there wasn't any money and he was looking at some considerable jail time, what was the point?

Of course I ran the risk of him shooting all of us out of despair. But maybe he'd give up. My arm was starting to get heavy too. We needed to end this soon.

"You idiot!" Mavis shrieked. "You didn't even find out if the job was legit!"

"She's lying!" was all Ted Dooley could think of to say.

"Why would I lie? I used to work for the CIA. I'm pretty up to speed on terrorists, domestic and foreign."

Okay, so I'd outed myself. I'd been doing that a lot lately. Why hide it anymore? My troop knew. Kelly and Rex knew. And I could spend time openly with my parents now.

Dr. Body's eyes grew wide. Really? That's what freaks her out in this whole showdown scenario? She knew Riley was CIA. Why did she think he was hanging out with me?

I could hear someone in an office behind Ted. Did he notice?

"So what's it going to be, Dooley?" I asked a little too loudly. I was trying to mask the noise.

"I'm not going to prison for this." The blood had returned to his face, and now it was red with rage.

He pulled the gun from Soo Jin's head and started to aim at me. I shoved his secretary, hard toward him, and her body blocked me from view. Ted stalled, unsure what to do, and I made good use of that time.

I couldn't shoot him in the chest or head. I'd risk shooting Dr. Body. So I aimed at an area that would do the least damage if I hit her. I aimed for his right leg. The bullet connected, and he screamed. Dr. Body dashed to the left and into the arms of Rex, who had been trying to sneak up behind Dooley.

Ted roared and brought his gun up toward me, and I dove for the floor. A gunshot rang out, and I looked up to see a very confused security director looking at a bloom of red in the middle of his chest, just before he fell over dead.

Standing behind him, gun still aimed, was Kevin.

CHAPTER TWENTY-TWO

———

I soon found out what had happened to Riley and Rex. After I'd found Ted, Riley was helping carry Evelyn's bomb to the bomb squad from Des Moines, who'd just arrived. And apparently, cutting the three red cords had been a bad idea, because that would've caused the bomb to explode immediately. Fortunately for us, Evelyn's…um…juices had corroded the bomb, effectively shutting it down. Oops.

Rex had searched the second floor and then checked the parking lot. There was only one car that didn't belong to anyone we knew. Rex called for backup, and when they arrived, Kevin recognized his father's car.

Apparently, Kevin wasn't very fond of his dad either. And he knew a way into the security office. He'd led Rex in and saved the day.

My father had conferred with the police department and Riley and called Agent Savage to let him know he was now going to be working the guard shack at the White House. As I came out into the parking lot, he was giving a statement to the media. And by media, I mean the *Who's There Observer*—our weekly paper, and local anchorwoman, Lucinda Schwartz. And her hair looked amazing.

"Mrs. Wrath?" Lauren was standing beside me. I didn't even see her walk up to me.

"Where's Mrs. Albers?" I asked as I scanned the lot. At the far corner were Kelly and the girls. I breathed a small sigh of relief.

"Can I keep the puzzle box?" Lauren asked. "As a memento? They wouldn't let me have the bomb."

"It might have to be entered into evidence." I patted her on the head. "But I'll see what I can do." I winked.

Lauren turned and joined the other girls, presumably to tell them she was getting a rather gruesome souvenir. I really should have thought that through, I realized, when several little heads turned to glare at me. I didn't have enough kittens to make this right.

Rex had led Dr. Body to a waiting ambulance. I thought it was kind of ironic that we had to call an ambulance to see to people at the hospital. But I kept this to myself.

"You did great," Rex said as he walked toward me. He stopped short of taking me into his arms. Probably because his officers were there.

"Thanks," I said. I was exhausted. My adrenaline was long gone. "What happened with Red and Blue?"

"They're in custody," Rex grinned. "SWAT shot them both. They're alive."

I filled him in on what Ted Dooley had said.

"The Feds are coming to take them away. I don't think we will really know what happened for a while."

I motioned to Kevin. "Is he going to be alright?"

Rex turned grim. "I don't know. He'll have to go through counseling just like any other officer who fires their gun in the line of duty. But with shooting his own father, I imagine it will take a little longer."

Kevin was surrounded by officers who were patting him on the back. He didn't respond. He just stood there, eating chips and dip. Where he got the food, I have no idea.

"Snails are fascinating creatures!" Bobbie, Lauren's mom, raved as we all sat on the floor in her basement.

True to her word, Bobbie had agreed to host the next troop meeting, and unfortunately, she knew more about snails than anyone should. Ever. Did you know that snails can have up to 14,000 teeth—and they're on their tongue? I didn't either. I probably could've gone all my life without knowing that, but there you go.

Oddly, the girls were enraptured. I wondered how much of this was because they were interested and how much was because they were getting a real tour of the morgue for the next meeting. Okay, so I'd told them if they weren't good, we couldn't do the morgue. Sue me.

"So," Kelly whispered in my ear, "snails."

I nodded. "Snails."

"How long before the girls want them as pets?" Kelly asked as she shifted Finn in her arms. Even the baby seemed transfixed.

Some girls are boy crazy. Some are girlie girls. Our troop was animal crazy. Any animal was awesome. Any. And right now, that included snails.

"I hear Soo Jin is picking up the kittens this weekend."

I felt a pang of regret. But after what that poor woman went through, I couldn't refuse. Of course Riley insisted. Again. Damn him.

"Yeah. It'll be quiet without Bond and Moneypenny," I mumbled.

Kelly said, "Two cats are fine. You don't need more than that."

I nodded. I'd made an appointment for Philby to get spayed. She didn't need any more diversions. And the pink was starting to wear off. Of course, it was wearing off on my bedspread. And my sofa. And the carpet. My bangs were even fading.

"And Riley?" Kelly asked as innocently as she could pull off.

"Riley's on a plane to DC."

And good riddance. Why did I think that? Who even says that anymore? Anyway, he had to go to Langley to file his report. He'd made some mutterings about retiring early and moving here, again. I told him that the Hotel Wrath was no longer open. He said something about Soo Jin's guest room that I wished I hadn't heard.

Red and Blue turned out to actually be from an Idaho militia. And they'd hired Evelyn to carry out an assignment. When she found out about the target—which really was the fertilizer plant in Willow Grove (I sent Agent Savage a box of donuts, and I might have rubbed his nose in it), she refused. Apparently, she'd voted for President Benson. And had no interest in blowing him up.

So, she fled to the nearest town of Who's There, Iowa and managed to attach herself to my trip with my troop. Once in DC, she'd planned to disappear. But apparently, she liked us and decided to stay. I wouldn't have guessed that in a million years.

When Red and Blue found out, they waited for her to resurface, which she did. It wasn't a smart move for her to stay in Who's There, but then I figured out by now that Evelyn wasn't very smart. She even tried to warn me when she found out my dad was going to be at the event. Weirdly, she liked him too. Red and Blue were outraged and decided to blow up my town instead. I still was iffy on how they recruited Ted Dooley, but an interview with Mavis indicated he'd been disgruntled for a while now because he'd never gotten into the police department as a young man. Kevin getting the job, with all of his worthlessness, drove him mad. So it was revenge. Sort of.

How did I know all of this? Because when I got home from the insanity at the hospital, I found a letter in my mailbox confessing everything. Of course, Evelyn ended it saying she was going to head south and I'd never see her again. That didn't turn out quite the way she'd planned it.

I was surprised that it took so long for a letter mailed from Who's There to Who's There to get to me. But oh well. Oh, and remember the fax Evelyn had sent to the CIA, implicating me should she turn up dead? Well, that was wrong too. Some jerk manning the fax machine wrote down the wrong thing. What she'd really said was to look for me *if* she turned up dead.

The newspaper found out who I really was and asked to do an interview. I've put them off but promised them a scoop when I was ready. I didn't really want to go back to being Finn Czrygy. I liked Merry Wrath.

I just needed a little more time to figure her out. I was looking forward to things getting quiet around here, spending time with my boyfriend, getting to know Soo Jin Body a little better, and spending some quality time with a faded pink cat who looked like Hitler, and her kitten, who looked like Elvis.

ABOUT THE AUTHOR

Leslie Langtry is the *USA Today* bestselling author of the *Greatest Hits Mysteries* series, *Sex, Lies, & Family Vacations*, *The Hanging Tree Tales* as Max Deimos, the *Merry Wrath Mysteries,* and several books she hasn't finished yet, because she's very lazy.

Leslie loves puppies and cake (but she will not share her cake with puppies) and thinks praying mantids make everything better. She lives with her family and assorted animals in the Midwest, where she is currently working on her next book and trying to learn to play the ukulele.

To learn more about Leslie, visit her online at:
http://www.leslielangtry.com

Enjoyed this book? Check out these other reads available in print now from Gemma Halliday Publishing:

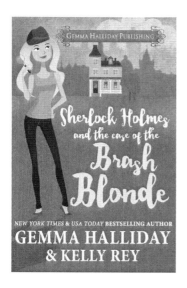

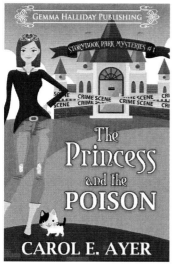

www.GemmaHallidayPublishing.com

Made in United States
North Haven, CT
01 June 2022

19752997R00121